STANLEY STEPANIC

Encyclopocalypse Publications
www.encyclopocalypse.com

Contents

A Vamp There Was

Middy Grove's Letter to His Sister   3
January 3rd, 1921

A Letter from Dorothy Kendall to Her Sister
Alma Tackett   8
January 12th, 1921

Middy Grove's Letter to His Sister   11
January 14th, 1921

Middy Grove's Letter to His Sister   17
January 22nd, 1921

The Free-Lance   28
January 25th, 1921 and November 2nd, 1922

Middy Grove's Letter to His Sister   30
March 13th, 1928

The Death of Mrs. Thomas C. Grove   31
March 1928

Middy Grove's Letter to His Sister   32
March 26th, 1928

Letter written in 1928, by Middy Grove   36

Historical Notes   69

The Path of the "Vamp"
An Essay by Stanley Stepanic

The Path of the "Vamp"   77

**Notable Vamps and the Vamp's Cultural
Impact in Film**

Josephine Baker   117
Freda Josephine Baker, née McDonald, 1906 – April 12, 1975

Theda Bara   122
Theodosia Burr Goodman, 1885 – 1955

Elisabeth Bergner   126
1897 – 1986

Olive Borden — 130
Olive Mary Borden, 1906 – 1947

Clara Bow — 134
Clara Gordon Bow, 1905 – 1965

Lili Damita — 138
Liliane Marie-Madeleine Carré, 1904 – 1994

Lya de Putti — 142
Amália Helena Mária Róza Putti, Putti Amália Helena Mária Róza, 1897 – 1931

Kay Francis — 146
Katharine Edwina Gibbs, 1905 – 1968

Greta Garbo — 150
Greta Lovisa Gustafsson, 1905 – 1990

Helen Louise Gardner — 154
1884 – 1968

Louise Glaum — 158
1888 – 1970

Jetta Goudal — 162
Julie Henriette Goudeket, 1891 – 1985

Barbara La Marr — 166
Reatha Dale Watson, 1896 – 1926

Myrna Loy — 170
Myrna Adele Williams, 1905 – 1993

Martha Mansfield — 174
Martha Ehrlich, 1899 – 1923

Nita Naldi — 178
Mary Nonna Dooley, 1894 – 1961

Pola Negri — 184
Barbara Apolonia Chalupec, 1897 – 1987

Asta Nielsen — 190
Asta Sofie Amalie Nielsen, 1881 – 1972

Anna May Wong — 196
Wong Liu Tsong, 黃柳霜, January 3, 1905 – February 3, 1961

Acknowledgments — 201
About the Author — 203
Image Credits — 205

For those whose soul still bleeds.

A VAMP
THERE WAS

The rear of the Pickle Factory photographed by Frances Benjamin Johnston between 1927 and 1929.

Middy Grove's Letter to His Sister, January 3rd, 1921

Sis,

How're things? Work's been good at the old pickle factory.[1] Ha. The weather was balmy this week the paper said. What a word. Balmy. Everyone thinks there's some crime wave in Fredericksburg now. There was this negro[2] who robbed a woman on Xmas Eve night,[3] how about that? But then, Goldsmith's was broken into too. Mrs. Backley told me all about it because she saw it happen. She was looking right at the store from her window in the dead of night. She happened to see two men, and one threw a brick through the glass of the front door. She ran yelling to her neighbor, since she don't have a telephone, and when they heard her the men ran out of Goldsmith's[4] and down the street but they got them later. They were US Marines the paper said, can you believe that? US Marines robbing Goldsmith's.[5] Different times. But it's like I heard someone say. It doesn't matter who you are or where you come from, some people are just bad. But that wasn't the most important thing.

I met a girl today. I remember I'd seen her before. First time she was down on Main[6] smoking a cigarette right outside of Bond's.[7] She doesn't dress like the other girls, not even the ones from the industrial up there on the hill,[8] so she's right out of a big city like what I seen in pictures. Has that bobbed hair even. Well, she was smoking, and I don't really like that, but anyway Dr. Bond came out and hollered at her about the gas pump or something. She gave him this glance and he just stood still like he was stuck. She walked away without saying a word. I thought that was odd.

So today I went to Goldsmith's because I wanted to see what those Marines done and I needed a new shirt anyway. Not much to see, the door only had the glass broken out. I was about to leave, but then she came right in, that girl did. I didn't even notice, at first, because I was there with Vern,[9] but then I heard humming and I remembered it was that song we used to listen to on the phonograph went something like "keep vamping till you vamp your cares away..."[10] When I heard that I looked, and there she was, that girl again, same one I saw outside of Bond's, humming that song.

I thought maybe she wanted to buy something for her daddy, cause she was walking all around the men's clothing humming and looking nowhere in particular. She had this coat hitting right above her knees and that bobbed hair,[11] but most of it covered with this hat that made her eyes look like they were all hidden in dark. Well, she caught me watching and turns her head at me with these strange eyes. I don't know quite how to explain it and maybe that's why the doc stopped the way he did that one day. Like she was looking into me. I felt just stuck there.

"Need something miss?" Mr. Goldsmith asks.

That shook me out of it, but the girl she looks at him and just says "No, just looking at what good men wear." She gave me and Vern a look, walked slowly to the door, and Mr. Goldsmith calls out to her "have a nice day now." She didn't even turn to say nothing back, just walks right out. Well, some man came up to buy some things and I heard Goldsmith say to him, "Girls like that are trouble." What do you think about that?

– *Middy*

A Letter from Dorothy Kendall to Her Sister Alma Tackett, January 12th, 1921

Dear Malma,

Vernon has been acting worse. He won't kiss me and even when I try to place a hand on him just to feel his shoulders he jerks away like I'm the flu. And he keeps staying late at the pickle place and it just doesn't make any sense you know? I don't think I could believe it myself but it's true what you said. He's seeing another woman. I just want the man I remember back I don't care what happened. I want how he used to come home from work and I'd have his dinner ready. I just want to sit and watch him eating and hear that sound he makes when he chews. He hasn't done that for days now. That's how I first knew something was really wrong. I even asked him about it and he yelled at me. Wasn't like him at all. He kept saying there's nothing going on and how could I think there was and other things like that. I was starting to think I was crazy and everything was just in my head. Went to town and did a little shopping like you said to do a little something for myself but it didn't help.

So I followed him after work today. My heart died when I saw her. She's so much better than me. I wish I wasn't so fat from going to Liberty all the time.[1] I wish I had something smart to say. I wish I could make him laugh more. I wish I wasn't just some plain old girl. What do I offer anyway? This girl has fashion. She has low heeled shoes I was thinking about buying the other day. Her hair is all bobbed and beautiful and she had these shining eyes. Can't say I blame Vernon after seeing her. Judging by appearances, I suppose I would say she's what folks call a flapper.[2] You've heard of the type? He was trying to follow her and was calling something, but she kept turning to him and yelling. She was trying to shoo him off like he did to me a few times. You'd have thought I'd like that, but I just wanted to run up to him and hold him. Can you believe that? Anyway, by that point they were walking down the street towards the hotel there, you remember it? We went to a dance there once me and him. You met him then. I had all these things in my head of how they were going in there and what was going to happen. You ever have that happen? These thoughts get in there like a fire and they won't go away. They just start burning up anything good. Any try you make to get them out of there they just get hotter and brighter. What a horrible feeling. It makes me shake to think about it. It was like I was losing all control of myself.

I walked a few feet away once they ducked into an alley and stood there staring at them. They didn't see me at first. He was talking to her close in what sounded a mean whisper. She seemed angry with him and was acting cold. He was whispering to her in a frenzy but I couldn't hear a word of it. I could just tell he was upset. Then the girl turns at me and it took my breath away. It was a stare I can't explain, but there was something sad in her eyes just for a moment once she realizes who I must be. As she's looking at me for that brief second Vernon turns to see what's going on and he goes white.

"Dorothy no, it's not..." he started, but the girl broke right into his words and pushed him to the side.

"You just shut up."

I was still looking like a scared cat and she walks right up to me and stares at me. I couldn't say a word to her. Maybe that or I'd slap her. I thought I would if it came to this but I couldn't. For a moment I saw that flash of sadness again somewhere deep in her eyes.

"Eh," she starts, "Don't you worry nothing 'bout this one, he ain't got nothing inside him I need. You keep him. I'm tired of his stammering, he's just getting in the way. I told him to scram. You keep him sweetie, maybe he'll do you better, but don't bet on it, no one ever changes," she said with that sad sort of look she made before.

When she walked past me I felt a light brushing of her hand on my shoulder. It felt like she was trying to calm me down. It was almost sweet but how can I say that? You'd have thought I'd have hit her there, but I didn't. I guess I didn't see anything when I think about it all and read everything I wrote so far, but I'm sure there were things from other times I'd never want to hear about. You can just tell, you know? Like there's this stink around people like that. Vernon and I, well, I don't know what we're going to do. He swore to me nothing happened between them but I wish I knew what that girl meant when she said to me he ain't got nothing inside. What did she mean? What do you think? Vernon is quiet sometimes now. He'll just be staring there out the window. Why I made his dinner hoping it would bring a little of him back, but he just pushed the plate away, stood up, and left the house. It's strange but him doing things like that makes me want to hug him. I was so angry some days but now I want nothing more than just to hold him. I just want to hold him. Should I come live with you awhile? Maybe he needs to see what it's like without me, maybe then he'll see I'm worth something. I'd like to think that he learned a lesson, that maybe he got close but had second thoughts. Even if something was happening between them I think it's over now. He didn't even know much about her, can you believe that? That's one thing I just can't fathom. How could someone do a thing like that without really knowing the person? I don't even think he knew her name. Should I come? Tell me what you think soon.

– Little Dorothy

Image as it appeared in *The History of the City of Fredericksburg, Virginia*,
By Silvanus Jackson Quinn, 1908.

Middy Grove's Letter to His Sister, January 14th, 1921

Sis,

Me again. I know I said I'd write more, so here. You know me, I do my work and I don't get into any trouble. Except this time I almost did. I thought about what you said in your letter about that girl I told you about and what you said about the Bible, and especially how that bobbed hair is getting everyone upset anymore. Why I just heard from Vern that he and his wife almost got into some trouble due to some girl with hair just like that. He wouldn't talk to me much and when I asked what was going on he looked down at the ground and I could hear Dorothy sobbing upstairs. I asked him what was wrong and he said she's just getting older and was a little jealous of some fancy girl trying to talk to him, nothing at all. They seem fine though, and he's a good man. I don't know women much. Well I guess I don't know them at all, but maybe I will soon. That girl I told you about had me all funny and just kept seeming to find me somehow.

I went to see that play Freckles[1] at the Opera House[2] I told you about. Heard someone say in the crowd before it started that it was a book. I never read it. You heard of it? Well, the play seemed good from the little I watched, so I'd guess the book is. It's about this orphan boy with no name, all on his own, and I kind of felt like that was me, seeing as how I'm on my own now, in the city here. That's right, I moved out. Got my own place there right in the city. Mama'll be fine. I know you don't want to hear about her, but I thought I should tell you. So the play looked real nice. They had this fancy set up with plants in the background and the best part was when Freckles meets this girl he called the Angel.[3] I thought to myself I would love to find a girl like that. Some girl that knows the world for what it is and knows how to live in it, and I just kept thinking about it as I watched.

Well, there she was, that girl again. She was sitting some rows up, but I knew it was her because I saw her head move and caught her face. It was dark in there while the play was on and I don't think she saw me then, but I saw her. After I did, to tell the truth, the play was like a breeze going by. The songs kept playing and I just kept looking at the back of her head, watching her, thinking about Freckles and his Angel even though the story was passing me by. When it was all over I wanted to talk to her but I saw she was with some fellow. He was older so it must be her daddy. I watched them go out and I don't know why but I followed them into the night.

The Highway Inn photographed by Frances Benjamin
Johnston between 1927 and 1929.

*They walked down Main. Remember how we used to do that
together? Still like it was, but things are changing too with all that
talk about the highway coming nearby.*[4] *They say they might even
get lights down the street.*[5] *Well, I followed them, and I stayed as far
behind as I could because I thought maybe I'd get an idea of where
she lived. They went up to Princess Anne and then took a turn past
the Highway Inn*[6] *to the houses there. Eventually, the man turned to
her and was looking around. They were talking about something
pretty loud, but I didn't want to get any closer. So I ducked behind
the corner of the inn. When I looked back around he was walking the
other way and she was coming towards me. I didn't know what to do,
so I just walked back where I came from and tried to act like I was
already there on the sidewalk doing my thing and walking along.*

*So, here the girl came, right behind me. I could hear her shoes
stamping on the sidewalk as she got closer and I thought to myself I
need to talk to her. She kept coming and then passed right by me,
hands in her coat pockets and her head kind of down. I was too
chicken to speak, but then got lucky. She was a bit ahead of me and*

then just stopped. I stopped myself, because she wasn't doing anything, just standing there with her back to me. Next thing I know, she turns and walks right up to me, puts her hand on my chest and pushes me against one of the pillars holding up the porch behind me.

"Why you keep following me around?" she asks.

I was tongue-tied, couldn't say nothing, just stood trying to think of some kind of words to say. Next thing I know, her head moves forwards and her eyes are looking straight into mine. I felt funny then, like there was something flapping around in my skull. Then, she brings her face even closer and I felt like I was going to faint. I didn't know what she was going to do, but suddenly she just backs up and puts her hands in her pockets, like nothing happened, and I felt fine again. She turned to walk away, but I mustered up some courage.

"What's your name?" I asked.

She stopped, turned, and walked right up to me, again with this anger in her face, but kind of nice like with this cute little smile. I started to back up and she stops.

"You ain't got nothing to ask me anymore. Talk to your friend, he can teach you a lesson or two 'bout me."

"What? Who?"

Then she gave me a look like I was some puppy dog that didn't listen good.

"That Vern of yours, you go ask him all about me. Don't yah remember? At Goldsmith's them weeks ago? Yeah, you ask him all about me maybe that will keep you out of my business."

I didn't get what she meant about Vern so I asked her then, feeling a little more brave.

"What about him? Why we both met you at the store, yeah, what's it matter? Just looking around, why we didn't say nothing to you."

She shook her head then.

"Just forget it."

"Why'd you leave your daddy back there? He seemed plenty mad."

"My daddy?"

"Yeah you was talking to him over there," I said, pointing back in the direction I saw her first, "And you both seemed real mad."

"My daddy?" she asks again with a smile kind of like the one she gave a few moments before.

"Yeah, that man back there, the one you were seeing that Freckles play with."

Then she just laughs and how loud it was. She seemed real happy then.

"Oh, my, yeah my daddy. You don't worry about my daddy he'll be fine. Too old anyway, sometimes, you know," she says glancing around, "He just don't work right anymore, know what I mean?"

"Oh yeah, mama's been getting that way for a while now. Sometimes she forgets things. But she's fine on her own that's why I moved out and all."

Then she laughs again.

"Oh you are a goof, ain't yah?"

"Goof? What you mean?"

Then she got mad again and looked around.

"Listen, I don't got time for this. Stay away from me, y' hear? Dry up.[7] You're too good for me."

That part got me, I didn't know what she meant. Me too good? I don't even think I have much to offer a girl like her. She could probably find any guy she wanted. Well, I kept my mouth shut and she just walks off, down the street into the night. Once she got past the light in the middle of the road I couldn't see anything, just heard her shoes stamping in the darkness until there was nothing. What do you think she meant by that, too good? She's different than any girl I seen before, like a firecracker. I think, like that Freckles, there's got to be someone for me out there and I got a feeling this is the gal. Makes me feel nice that she thinks something of me, to say something like that, and she don't even know me. What do you think? Forget that Bible stuff, you're a girl, you got to know something about these things. What does her hair really matter anyway? She seems like she's a fine young girl to me. Maybe if she's still smoking I can get her to quit it. And tell me all about that snow you got up there in Roanoke, too. Paper said it was 18 inches![8]

– Middy

Middy Grove's Letter to His Sister, January 22nd, 1921

Sis,

Well, I did what you said and avoided that girl. I even talked to Vern while we were working at the factory about her but at first he said he didn't even remember no girl from Goldsmith's at all. So I said to him:

"You know, that girl with the bobbed hair we saw that day after those Marines busted the window."

That got him for some reason because he looked up at me real quick and looked mad.

"Wait, this that girl I've heard you going on about now and then?"

"Yeah, same girl."

"What's her name? What you know about her?" he started to ask real quick.

"Why, I don't know much of nothing about her, just saw her about was all. Thought she might like to talk, you know, maybe some company."

Then his eyes were darting around and he looks at me again, almost looking scared.

"What she say? Why you talking about her?"

"Just talking that's it. I just been seeing her around now and then that's all. I just thought she looked like a girl I might need to get to know. Saw her at that play I told you about the other day and..."

"You just stay away from her!" he snaps at me, then catches himself when he saw some people looking at us.

Then he gets into this whisper.

"Listen, Mid, remember what Mr. Goldsmith said that day?"

"I thought you didn't remember no girl."

"Nah, I'm talking about what he said. Forget that girl. It's any girls like that. Girls like that are trouble, you just stay away from her, you hear me? Almost ruined Dorothy and me a girl like that. You just stay away from her."

"Well what's it matter? You said you just talked to some girl like that and Dorothy just got a little uptight about it. Just talking. That's all I'm doing."

"It ain't just talking!" he started to raise his voice.

"What you mean?"

"Mid, just forget it. You just stick to the girls around here. Ain't nothing you need from a girl like that, you understand?"

Well I saw he was getting upset so I didn't want to talk anymore about it.

"Yeah, yeah Vern, I get it. I'll forget all about it."

For a moment there Vern looked like he was going to say something else, why he almost seemed mad at me. But then he shook his head and said we should get back to work. I don't know what that girl was saying to me that other day on the street about me needing to talk to Vern. I just won't bother in their business anyway because what's my girl got to do with it? It seemed to make him mad so must have reminded him about something. Only thing I can figure is she must have known the girl that had Dorothy all upset. If Vern wants to talk about it again well I'll let him do it. And what's my business is my business.

Anyway, after going to some preaching like you said I should, I've been thinking more about all of it. Maybe it was supposed to be this way, me and that girl. Let me tell you what I mean. After what you said in your letter, well, I thought about it. I know you don't like me talking about mama that much, but I told her all about it too and she said the same thing, that girls like that are trouble. And I thought about what Vern said too. So, I went there to hear that preacher, like you said I should, since I hadn't been in a while, and they've been having a revival going on. I went on Tuesday. I said, well, let me see *if I can forget about this girl and see what God has to say about her. Maybe he knows something because I can't make sense out of Vern or what I'm thinking so let's see what the man up there has to say.*

I went to that one church there on Hanover and a Reverend Hout was preaching.[1] I walked on down the street there from the factory, and the ice was creeping up the banks from all the cold we been having. There was big chunks of it coming down from up north somewhere. So, I got to that church. There was lots of singing and this Hout was talking on and on about gates, about how the good path is narrow and the gates are different. Most people, he says, they go on through the broad gate, but there's another one. He says, people, they're stuck between both. They got some goodness, they got some badness. He says the Christian life ain't meant to be easy and we all need God.

That got me thinking about that girl again. I seen her at least twice, since the last letter I sent you, but I did what you said and kept away. But sitting there, listening to that preaching, thinking about what Vern said, I notice there's someone over and in front of me a ways and they ain't standing or singing. I was wondering why and then I could tell by the hair it was her. After that, I didn't hear much of anything. I just kept looking at her. Everyone was singing, clapping, saying their prayers, and she just sat there not moved by any of it. Eventually, she turns her head and sees me. She just looks at me, doesn't move her eyes, doesn't give no sort of move-ment. But then she smiles, and what a smile. It was like she was saying to me with that smile, "what, you ain't listening to none of this neither?" I remembered what she said to me about being good and how you, Vern, and mama said those kinds of girls was no good. And there's that Reverend Hout going on about paths in life. All that wickedness, the vile and vicious things in mankind. I thought about those Marines breaking into Goldsmith's and there was that girl looking at me, just at me, and smiling. I said to myself, well, that's my Angel right there, just like Freckles. That smile is nothing but what I need. God must have been telling me something after all.

So, I made up my mind, I was going to talk to her after the preaching. Once it was over, everyone started talking and moving, and I almost lost sight of her. I went through the crowd, and then I seen her leaving with her coat and hat on, all alone. I went out of that church and followed her down the stairs. She stops there at the bottom and turns to me like she knew I was coming like that one day on the street, her eyes looking all shiny under the brim of that hat.

"You still following me around, after I told you to scram? You talk to your friend?" she asks me.

"Yeah Vern don't know nothing about you. Didn't even remember when we saw you at Goldsmith's."

"Yeah, sure, never would..." she started to say and then stopped.

"What's your name?" I asked, because I knew it was my chance.

"What's it matter..." she says, turning to walk away.

Well, I was still brave, so I walked right up beside her and started talking.

"I see you around a lot, and well, since you're alone tonight, thought you might like someone to walk you home."

"Want me to be under your arm, do ya? What you gonna do, when you get me home?" she asks with this teasing look.

"Walk you to the door."

"Uh huh," she says, "Then what? I serve yah some of my straw-berry preserves?"

"Oh, I wouldn't come in for that, unless you asked me."

Then she gives this laugh that echoes off the buildings.

"You really do mean strawberries, don't yah? Well, you listen, I'm done with this place now, just seeing what it was about in there, down in this Bible Belt pit. I like to hear them talk sometimes. Reminds me about what I'm doing. This is my last night."

"What was you seeing about in there?"

She looked at someone passing us a moment and smirked.

"Church. Preaching. All those people acting like they're so full of goodness, cause they sitting pretty in there, like they're on that narrow path he was talking about. They're all liars, dirty, filthy things. They don't deserve the skin they're wearing any more than the coats that warm 'em. That one there with his wife," she says pointing at this man coming down the stairs, "He'd do anything for a girl like me, he'd leave everything behind. He'd do things to me that would make old women swoon, just because he wants to feel alive, like he's still somethin'. Just like that damn Vern of yours. Doesn't want to be dead, doesn't want to know it's coming, like it comes for all of you. So, he looks for a girl like me."

I didn't know what she was on about.

"What're you talking about? Vern don't know anything about you."

"Course he don't, ha!"

"There some girl you know or something? He told me his wife was mighty upset about this girl he was talking to but weren't nothing more than that from what I gathered."

She smiled this gentle way, but stayed silent, so I kept talking like I do.

"So what you talking about filthy people? What'd you mean?"

"Nothing, I told you, you're too good for me, beat it kid," and she starts to turn.

"Kid? Why, you and me look about the same age, if I'm a kid well so're you."

She smiled at that.

"I'm not a kid."

"I ain't either."

She gave another laugh, and it was so sweet.

"You're a funny one, you don't know nothing about what those people are thinking in there. And it seems hard to believe, but you really don't know much about anyone. You're just a regular guy. First time for everything I suppose."

That one confused me.

"Just look at you. Ha! Thinking I want you to eat strawberry jam with some crackers. Real funny thing you carryin' a torch for me."[2]

"Torch? I don't get..."

"Just some city talk country goof. Listen, fine, you want to talk to me and walk some, to no particular place, go ahead then."

"Don't you need to go home?"

She looks over at that man she pointed at earlier, who was getting close to us. The woman he was with, I guess his wife the way she was holding onto his arm, well she sees me and the girl standing there and her eyes go real wide. She looked like she was going to say something or maybe was a little pale in the face. Then I feel that girl tugging on my sleeve.

"No home for me anywhere, just walk, got it? Get me away from these people, last thing I need is to hear yellin'," and she points ahead into the dark.

I wanted to ask what she meant, but I just nodded. We start walking, and I was talking her head off like I did at home all the time when you were around and everything was still fine with mama. Didn't say much about herself, though. Sometimes she used funny words and I didn't know what she meant. Some of them sounded like how grammy used to talk, but most were real new city talk. I liked how she just listened to me, just walked and let me go on about a whole lot of nothing. She even looked up and smiled a few times. That made me feel good. Next thing I know, I'm talking, and she puts her arm into mine and just holds on there as we walk. About then I was going to ask her what she does or what she likes to do, when that man she pointed to earlier and his wife passed us. I guess on their way home but I'm not too sure why they came back the way they came. They looked like they were talking about something important. He turned his head and he gives me this worried look. Then I see his wife, who was walking silent, look up at him and then she turns to us. She gets that same look on her face I saw when they passed us earlier.

"You would be there!" she screams.

I couldn't believe it, she just comes up and slaps my Angel, on the side of the face, and I didn't even know her name yet, just thought of her that way. That man comes over and he grabs his wife and he's yelling at her and she's yelling back at him, about how he ruined everything and no amount of preaching is going to do no good for either of them. And she's screaming and pointing at the Angel saying she ruined everything and I didn't know what any of it was about. Well, the Angel, she's laughing with her hands on her hips. The man, he's trying to pull his wife away, and she's crying and yelling, and when he turns again, I remembered his face. Why he was the same one talking to old Mr. Goldsmith that one day I saw the Angel in the store when me and Vern was there. Next thing I know, I feel this hand grip my wrist like a vice,[3] and it's her. Real strong hand.

"Guess we gotta go now, people are gonna start looking. The less faces that remember me, the better."

She pulls me off to the one side of the street, and we go to the other, this motorcar almost running into us and honking its horn. She laughed and takes my arm again as we start running a short ways. We leave behind all that commotion and make our way down to Main and there's nobody around. Just us two, walking that street alone. I had to know what was going on.

"What was all that?" I asked.

"Nothing, don't you worry about it. I tell you a bit and you never get a clue, cause you're a good one."

"What's that mean anyway?"

She smiled.

"Just do your talking."

So I started up again going on about some old thing. Not even sure how long I talked or how long we were walking. However long it was, I notice she's looking kind of distant like she was thinking about something that made her sad. Then she starts talking in the middle of my rambling.

"You know," she says, "When I see their faces sometimes, like we did tonight, I think about myself. Like Dorothy."

"Wait, why, hold on, you mean Vern's Dorothy?"

"Eh, forget it. What I'm saying is that's maybe the one thing I don't like about it all. Don't like to see that look in their faces, in their eyes. I know what it feels like. I know it well."

"What's that? What do you mean? Who?"

"Like that woman back there. Know what it's like to want someone and not be wanted back. What it's like when they're thinking about someone else when you're sitting right there. You reach out for them and...never mind, forget it. In the end, in spite of me, those men have to make the decision to do what they do. I don't force it out of them, just give them the chance. They'd find it somewhere else if not for me. I'm just like a force of nature when it comes down to it."

Well I didn't know what she was saying, like she was stuck in some thoughts only she understood.

"What you mean?"

"Nothing, just what I said and here you are letting it run right past you. You just don't get it, it's not what you are, and you keep it that way. You're better off the way you are, don't change it. You listen to me now," she says, letting go of my arm as she stands in front of me, giving me a quick poke in my chest, "You forget all about me. You go find yourself a girl on that narrow path, if there is one, and you stay on there, you hear me? Don't you be following me around anymore, I'm through. I'm all done here, ain't nothing you need to worry about. I'm going to go the other way, and I don't want you following. You get behind me, I swear, I'll ruin you. You get me?" she asks, pointing and then poking me in the chest again.

I was confused, so I just nod at her, and she smiles, then gives me a kiss on my cheek.

"You're too good for me. You stay that way with your strawberry preserves."

She turns to leave, lighting up a cigarette, but I just couldn't let it end at that.

"I never knew your name. What's your name?"

She turns one more time, a cigarette hanging off her lip with its tip glowing in the dark.

"I don't need a name. Just a girl passing through. You leave me alone now, you'll read all about me soon. You find yourself a gal who's living. Forget all about me, you go on your way now, get going. You get going and do what I say. Go chase yourself now."[4]

I just watched her walk away then, because I had a bad feeling cause of what she said about being through. You probably were thinking up till now, oh Lord, what's that boy done this time, I told him, but it all turned out alright. Never liked a girl smoking. When she lit that old thing up it was like, for at least a bit, she didn't seem like the same girl. Strange because I do recall seeing her smoke before, but there was just something about all that talking we did together and then seeing her doing it again. That must've been God saying to me you look now and watch this one, you see, she's real trouble. I looked down Main, all dark, and I thought there she goes down there. I could hear her shoes clacking on the sidewalk, catching just a bit of her cigarette in the dark, till there wasn't anything but the shadows and that cracking ice on the river in my ears. Something about that girl's just wrong, you were right. I guess Vern was right too, and mama. That girl's gone through that broad gate to where there ain't no lights I bet. I'll come real soon to visit you don't you worry about me now.

– Middy

An Article in *The Free-Lance*, January 25th, 1921

YOUNG WOMAN SUICIDES
Ends Life by Jumping from Bradford Building[1]
NO KNOWN RELATIONS IN CITY

The Bradford Building, one of the few areas with a street light in
Fredericksburg, circa 1920.

JAN 23rd – A young woman was found dead early Sunday
morning, having jumped from the top of the Bradford
Building. The young woman's badly mangled body was
found on the sidewalk off of Commerce Street and her fall
snapped electrical wires, causing a small outage for those
nearby. Local resident Charles Pool, who was walking down
the street, noticed the woman on top of the building.

"She spread her arms like an angel and just jumped. She
just jumped right off of there. When she went through the
wires, there was an explosion," Pool said.

Police were curious how the young woman made it to the top. The fire escape was up and is currently being repaired. Aside from the impossible feat of scaling the walls there did not seem to be any way of making the climb. She was found in expensive clothing but had no clues about her identity. Fredericksburg police are hoping a family member will come forward.

A Wedding Announcement in *The Free-Lance,* November 2nd, 1922

Grove – Jones

A pretty marriage took place at the Methodist Episcopal Church, South last Saturday evening, when Miss Sallie Jones, daughter of blacksmith Walter Jones, became the bride of Middy Grove. Rev. Hout performed the ceremony. The young couple intends on moving to Richmond, after a short honeymoon to Belvedere Beach.[2]

Middy Grove's Letter to His Sister, March 13th, 1928

Sis,

I know you two haven't spoken in quite a while, and I know even I haven't been up to visit you in a long time, but Aunt Hannah said she sent you a letter and never heard back, so I wanted to make sure I sent something myself, because I know you'll write to me. I hope it won't make you cross. Mama's bad off. I don't think she's going to be around too much longer and it might be good if you came to see her before she goes. I think that would be real nice. I'm going to leave Sallie and the kids at home to help mama around the house for a spell, to see if she recovers, but I think this may be her last few weeks. Please write as soon as you can. You can send me a telegram at the station if you want. I will pay you for it later.

Yours,
Middy

An Obituary from *The Free-Lance*, March 23rd, 1928

Mrs. Thomas C. Grove Dead[1]

Funeral services for Mrs. Thomas C. Grove were held at her home this Sunday. Mrs. Grove was well-known and loved in the city and famous for her strawberry preserves. Mrs. Grove died peacefully in her home, after a long illness. She was watched over by friends and family. Mrs. Grove is survived by two children, Middy P. Grove and Miss Ida Grace Grove, and one sister, Mrs. Harry Jackson. Reverend Hout of the Methodist Episcopal Church, South officiated. Burial was in the City Cemetery.[2]

A Telegram from Middy Grove to His Wife, March 24th, 1928

To Mrs. Middy Grove

Fredericksburg, Va.

Mama dead. Need to stay around town to see to things. Vern helping. Let you know when I leave. Tell kids love them. See you soon. Love.

Middy

Middy Grove's Letter to His Sister, March 26th, 1928

Sis,

Wish you were here. I'm not sure what to think about it, but remember that girl from some years back I told you about? The one who jumped off the skyscraper? Well, I can't believe it, but I tell you I saw her in the city walking around. I never a forget face. I'm going to see if I can find out more about this, it all seems too strange to me. I know, I know, but I just got to do this.

Middy

A Letter Given to Mrs. Middy Grove by Her Husband on January 21st, 1968, Opened after His Death

Dear,

If you're reading this, it means I'm no longer with you. I'm sorry it took so long for you to hear all this, but I didn't have the words to tell you in person. Not sure where I could even begin. You would have thought I was crazy. Now, you don't have anything to worry about, what you're going to hear is all true, but there was nothing with me and this girl I'm going to tell you about. I would have told you sooner, but I couldn't. I just wanted to give you a good life. I think I succeeded in that regard and if I didn't, in any way, I'm sorry, but I don't think you'll think that. This is about my going home when mama died. Remember how you wondered at my way of acting when I got back? How I didn't like hearing the word angel? How I didn't seem to want to talk about the funeral, like how I talk about everything? Remember how I seemed to watch over the kids too much, especially Josie? Well, there's bad people out there in the world. I'll tell you what I mean. The letter included with this one is old. I wrote it back then. I read through it a hundred times, and I still don't know what to think, but I want you to know I loved you dearly, please forgive me if this causes you any pain, I always stayed true. I just couldn't find the way to tell you all of this. I still don't know myself what I saw. I'll be seeing you when you cross over. Maybe it will make sense then, to both of us. Don't bother putting flowers on my grave, you use that money for yourself.

Letter written in 1928, by Middy Grove

May 11th 1928

*When mama died and I came home I walked all around looking at
the old city. Who wouldn't? It's been five years since we been here. So
many motorcars now. It's strange seeing them on the streets at night,
and speaking of that you have street lights too. Why, I even saw the
girls school up there had some lights on its sidewalks.[1] Times change.
Place even has a new name now they call it the Teachers College. I
remember when the old gas light outside St. George's[2] used to make
me wonder what we'd see next. Well, I don't want to see much
anymore of this place after all that happened.*

*Mama was ready, it was her time and all. She was happy to see
me. Of course, you know Sis, she never came, but I promised mama
I'd make sure I kept talking to her, seeing her through whatever it is
she's going through. It was fairly uneventful. I expected I'd be home
soon enough. But that night, before mama died, I couldn't believe it,
but I saw someone I haven't thought about in years. I never told you
about her, but before I met you I met this girl in the city here many
years back. She was from somewhere else, some big city, I never found
out where. I saw her once near Bond's, then again at Goldsmith's,
humming this old song Sis and I used to listen to on record about this
woman called the Vamp. Remember that old picture we saw you and
I that one time? Anyway, I had a thing for that girl and I started to
try to get up the courage to say something to her, after I noticed how
fancy she was. Liked her so damn much I called her the Angel,
because of this play I saw. She told me to stay away, but I didn't. She
said to me "you're too good for me." Never knew what she meant by
that until later.*

One night back then I went to this revival at the church you and

I were married at, and I saw her there. She walked with me that time on the streets and listened to me go on about the city. Then, this man and his wife got in a scuffle over her and we got out of there. Before she left that time, she tells me again like she did before, "you're too good for me," and she tells me never talk to her again. And I didn't. Last thing she said was I'd read all about her. She was right about that, because she jumped off the skyscraper soon after and killed herself. I read about it in the paper. I always wondered what was on her mind, why she did it. I thought maybe I should have done something, tell the police what I knew, but I didn't know nothing about her actually. Now I do.

So, the night before mama died, she says to me, "Middy go out and walk, get some air, maybe go see that friend of yours. You been worrying too much about me, it's my time and that's all there is to it." So, I went. Not to see Vern, I didn't feel up to it. He'd been a big help with all this business and it was nice seeing him and Dorothy smiling together, but I just wanted to be alone. I just walked. There were some people out, wasn't that late. I took a walk down Main to see the sights I hadn't seen in a few years and then I heard this humming. I knew I had heard it somewhere before, and there it was. That same song I remembered about this woman called the Vamp. Same one that girl I called the Angel was humming when I saw her at Goldsmith's all those years ago.

When I heard that humming it was like I was sent back in time. I froze, then started looking around, and there she was, that same girl. She just passed by on the other side of the street and was going in the other direction. Now, I didn't think it could be her then, just some coincidence. There was no way it could be her, I thought, because I heard what happened to her. She jumped off that building and there's no coming back from that. Well, I watched her walk away, couldn't see who it was, and I just had to know. Some part of me had to know it wasn't her, so I followed.

Suddenly, she turns off the street onto a dirt road. I run up, go around the corner, and there she is, waiting for me and staring. Her eyes were just glowing there, or seemed like it, in the dark. There was no mistaking when I saw them. It was her, just like I last saw her. I remembered everything about her, and what shocked me most was she didn't look any different, just different clothes. It looked like nothing had changed and like she had just skipped some years and fell right in front of me humming that song I heard before.

"I told you to stop following me, and what you still doing here in this bumpkin village? Ain't no one remembered me so far, and here we go again with your foolery. Let's see what you are now."

Before I could say something, she comes up to me and leans her searing eyes into me, staring at me. I get this funny feeling again like when I first met her. Now, I better explain that. I don't mean that I liked her. I mean, I did, back then when we first met, but the feeling I'm talking about wasn't like that. It was like I was stuck and there was this feeling in my head, like something fluttering in my eyes and at the insides of my skull. Felt like fingers or wings in there touching on everything. Then it stops, and she leans back.

"Hmm, ain't that a surprise? Still a real strawberry boy. But forget it, your mama's dying. You best go to her, then back home to your family. You stay away from me, goof.[3] I'm going to have to leave these parts again for a time if I have to deal with you again and that'll ruin everything. I told you to beat it all those years ago and here you are again chasin' after me but wanting real strawberries like before. Just a goof."

She walks forwards then and puts a finger right in my chest near my heart.

"If you don't leave me be, this time I'm gonna bump you off like I said I would."

I was too scared to say anything, so I did what she said, I just left fast as I could and went back home. For some reason, I believed then what she said. Mama could tell I was shook up, but of course, she thought it was because of her being so close to death.

"It's just my time, I told you, just my time," she says to me.

Lucky for me, she wouldn't have any idea what I saw and I knew no one would believe it. After the funeral, I just couldn't come home to you at first. There were things to arrange and we had to figure what to do with the house. I needed to ask Sis about it too. There was lots to do. Vern was a big help. Helped get mama to the cemetery and clean up after the luncheon. He could tell there was something wrong with me, but that was easy to explain, just had to say it was the funeral and all of the how to do. But that girl was the problem. I couldn't figure it out and I wasn't leaving until I did. It had to be someone else, I thought, some other girl. Had to be some confusion. So, I was determined to know. I walked on the streets during the day, some at night. I caught a quick glimpse of her once walking along with this older gentleman near Goolrick's. I didn't want to bother her then. Well, if it was all just some misunderstanding, perhaps that man is her brother, maybe something like that, and I didn't want to make her mad because what if she meant what she said?

I was at the end of my rope, not sure what to do. How was I going to find her in all those people around there then? All those cars and sounds. Getting to be like Richmond, I thought. Well, one night I saw her by chance, walking down Princess Anne with some man, might have been the same one from the other day, so I followed her. I knew she knew I was there, because at one point she looked back at me. She didn't seem mad though, she must've known I wanted to know more about her. She knew I knew there was something strange about her, I just didn't know yet what it was and she must've known I wasn't going to be no threat to her. I don't know why she wanted to keep me away, but, well no I do now I suppose. Wanted to me to stay just the way I was for always. Didn't want me to know everything. That's probably it.

Postcard from approximately 1920 to 1926 of the Princess Anne Hotel.

She took that man into the hotel off Princess Anne.[4] *Strange to say, I had never been in there until then. Even Vern had been there, that's where he met Dorothy. I stayed back, watched the man and the Angel at the counter as she took out one of her cigarettes and smoked it while looking at a plant in the lobby. She glanced at me through some of the smoke, then he comes over to her, and she goes with him up the stairs, so I followed. When I got up there I went around the corner, carefully, and I see her standing outside an open door of one of the rooms. Just then, she stops and turns her head slowly. She looks at me and she smiles. It was a strange smile. Something wicked about it. She puts up a finger on her lips like to say "ssh" and, then I see this hand come out of the room and grab her by her coat, pulling her in gently, and as her face disappears she's still looking at me and smiling. When I saw that I went home because I didn't want to know what was going on in there. I knew it was no good. All the things she said to me the times before made sense then. I don't know why but they did just with that one little gesture. I thought about Vern again and some things she had said about him and I felt even worse. Was this the girl he talked about that had Dorothy upset? What did he do?*

I was all alone that night feeling that way, everything was all done. All living family had gone home, friends were gone, and mama was in the grave. I tried to sleep up in there in my old room, then the couch, even the floor. Just couldn't do it. Couldn't sleep anywhere. So, I went out again and didn't even put my coat on, though it was colder than usual. Part of me, some small part, is glad I did. The rest, though, just wishes I left it all behind me.

I went back to that hotel to see if I couldn't see something. I still don't know what really drew me there again. Should have stayed away. It was late then, not much of anyone about on the street. Eventually, after waiting who knows how long and all cold, I see that girl coming out of the hotel. She was kind of rushing, like she was getting away from someone. Then, I see that gentleman coming out and he's yelling at her. A couple watched them briefly, talked to themselves, and then went inside. The girl just kept walking, and he comes up to her and starts pulling at her coat. Well, she pushes him off and runs across the street. When I started getting closer I heard a few things.

"You ruined me...you come back here...come back here..."

I followed them and they go into this alley there. I come up to the side of the alley, listening, and there was this barrel on the ground, like one of the ones from the old pickle factory where I worked. With that, I could get low and see around through a little crack between it and the wall. So, I see them there arguing in the alley and I can hear everything. This man, he's going on and on about how she ruined his life. How he gave up everything for her. I thought of the woman she fought with on the street after the preaching that one night when I saw her at the church. But it was hard to focus on my thoughts because they kept on yelling.

"I don't care what you did, I told you, you ain't nothing to me, no better than any other," she says.

"I gave up my wife, my children, my money, I gave it all up for you! All of it."

It was then I thought about Vern again and wondered if it was true, if he could do such a thing, and I remembered Dorothy crying that one time, but the arguing broke me from thinking again.

"You gave up nothing, they're still there at home."

"You think they want me around now?"

The girl she just smirks and sniffs.

"I told you I was trouble, but you wanted all of me, so you got it, and then you got what was coming to you, that's all there is to it."

"Just come back with me, stay with me there, could...could you hold me? I need..."

"I ain't staying with you no more, I told you I got what I need, I'm all done now. I got to go."

"You're far from done! You think we're through?!"

Next thing I know, he pulls out this pistol. His hands are shaking and he's pointing it at her, but she's just standing there like she ain't feeling a thing. I couldn't believe it then, still don't, but she just laughs at him and taps on the barrel and he puts it down.[5]

"Oh, what, you're going to bump me off? This pistol's more man than you anyway. And I like it cold."

Well, that made him mad and he brought the pistol back up, but she doesn't do nothing but smile. She just didn't care.

"Nothing to hide now, don't matter, so go ahead, go ahead and do it, shoot me, I want you to."

Then she leans into him, takes the gun and puts the barrel on her chest.

"Go ahead, shoot me, I'll enjoy it. I'm sure your family would too."

Next thing I know, there's a bang with a flash. My ears were ringing a bit but I could hear how she made this horrible choking sound and her body's falling back against the wall. I couldn't believe it, he shot her. So, he's standing there and I hear commotion behind me as my ears got clear again and turn to see someone coming out of the hotel and a light go on in a house down a ways. When I look back at the man, he's all shaking, and the pistol's still in his hand. He looks around, leans his head back and then takes the barrel to his chin and just as fast shoots himself. He fell over like a puppet that had its strings cut.

I was stunned, didn't know what to do or where I should go. But, for some reason, part of me still wanted to know about that girl, and I don't know why, but I went into that alley even though there were more people screaming and commotion getting near. I came up to her, skirting the puddle of blood coming out around her like a halo, and leaned down to look, just to see if maybe it was someone else. I didn't want to touch her head, because it was tilted, and there was a hole in the back of her coat. I heard some more commotion. There was someone yelling and pointing into the alley, just a shadow to me, but they ran away. Don't think they saw who I was at all, but I got scared.

Right when I was about to run, I heard this hissing breath and a groan and felt something grab a hold of my shirt. I look down, not believing what I'm seeing, and it's her. She pulls herself up off the ground a little ways, one hand holding onto me and she's starting to stand. There was blood coming out of her mouth and her eyes were blazing. I remembered how they seemed to glow to me in the dark the night she jumped off the skyscraper but this was like a fire was burning in them.

"Get me the hell out of here, you sap! Get me out of here, go."

"I need to...need to take you to the Mary Washington..."[6]

"Don't futz around. Forget the damn hospital. You got a place here, you take me there. Your mama's house."

I started to talk, but it was all a mumble.

"Stop beatin' your gums!" she screams, and coughs up some blood.

So she pulls herself up more and I manage to get her onto my shoulder and I find she's walking a bit on her own. I didn't know how. I thought I heard people getting close.

"We need to get you to the doctor's, to the…"

"I said take me to your damn mama's house, and do it before I snuff you out like I said I would. Go down the damn alley the other way, do it!" she finishes, grabbing me by my shirt.

Felt like she could have tossed me aside like a doll.So, I did what she said, we got out of that alley. With that man's body there, they didn't come looking for us at all I guess. Not sure they even saw her in there, whoever it was that looked into the alley. So, us two, we kept to the dark as much as we could, watching out for cars, people, and lights, and slowly made the way back to mama's. I look back and see there's some blood coming out of her dripping on the road.

"Don't worry about it, stuff will dry up like dust in a little while, keep going goof."

I didn't know what she meant. When we're nearing closer to mama's, me dragging her partially along in the dark and she gasping for air, I hear someone coming up. God, I thought, what next?

"Mid, what you doing?"

It was Vern, damn it to hell. What's he doing here, I wondered?

"Who's that, why you ain't home? I went by to see if you was…"

"That's where I'm going. I got to get her there."

"Is that…"

I look up and his eyes are wide.

"Is that blood? God man, what did you do to her?!"

"Nothing, she…"

Her head was still hanging down and there's this blood running down the front of her but she was talking just fine.

"Just fell down was all, get the hell out of here you damn fool, let me be."

I was standing there dumb holding on to her.

"*That weren't from no fall. What'd you do to her I said?!*" *Vern starts, and he pushes me.*

Her face comes up looking at him like some demon.

"*Wasn't him, you shut the hell up. Just a nasty cut, go back to your Dorothy, leave us be.*"

"*Leave her out of this, I told you that…*"

"*Don't need you around here, scram. Told you to beat it years ago! Go back to your Dorothy, didn't you hear what I said? Go back to her!*" *she yells to him.*

"*I ain't going nowhere,*" *Vern says, taking her by the other arm.*

"*I said I don't need yah! Your body ain't got what I need. Don't you get it? She's the one what wants you isn't that enough?! Isn't she enough?! Go back to her! Get!*"

Vern looked confused, or maybe, not sure, hurt but then he insisted and took hold of her anyway. She didn't fuss after he started to help and we made it back to mama's. Not sure how we did that exactly without anyone seeing us. We bring her inside to the parlor there where we had mama lying out for the funeral,[7] and she walks over and sits in our old green chair there near the fireplace, blood on her chest. She coughed and I saw blood on her hand. Funny thing was she was smiling as she looked at it. Me and Vern were just staring at her for a moment and she's looking at us.

"*What?*" *she asks, giving a smile,* "*Never seen a girl bleed before? I bet you didn't.*"

Vern keeps staring at her as he talks to me.

"*She must be in shock. I mean…she can't be too bad off if she's talking and smiling there, but that's got to be looked at. That…that can't just be no cut.*"

"*You wanna see it?*" *she asks him.*

Vern gave her an odd look, then turned back to me. I heard her give another wet cough and all this blood came sputtering out of her mouth.

"Mid, we can't leave her like this, we need to take her over there to the hospital. We gotta call 'em."

"Mama ain't got no phone. Never liked the things."

"Well, I gotta go call someone."

He turns to her.

"Listen, you know...I know the last time we talked it was...well. I think we need to think about things, you know? I can leave like I said, I'll do it... I told you before I wanted to move on and you, well, you're the girl. I think it's time I let Dorothy know that you and..."

I didn't understand what he was saying just then but when I look at her she seemed shocked, like she couldn't believe what she was hearing. She gives a little laugh.

"You really still on about that old stuff in the middle of all of this?" she asks as she holds her hand up, covered in her blood.

"I told you before, you're the girl."

Then she was mad, I could see it in her face, but she gave this sly smile.

"Ah, yes, that's right, isn't it? Get over here sweetie," she says to Vern.

"Now, I know what happened back then. But it's fate I found you like this, and you know I...we got to..." he starts to say, as he comes up to her sitting on that chair.

Next thing I know, she leaps up and bites down on his throat like a rabid wolf making this horrible growl or scream. Vern tries to fight her off, but he can't and he falls to the floor. I remember I used to see him moving around pickle barrels like they were babies and this girl he can't even budge. When he's on the floor he starts flailing and she's holding on to him. It was like a boulder holding him down, he just couldn't move her. I'm just standing there. Vern's struggling, she's still holding onto his throat with her teeth, right over his Adam's apple, and soon he's not moving as much, and then he's not moving at all. She stays on him for a bit longer, and then opens her mouth. I saw there was some blood on her teeth and there was a set of bruises with blood all over Vern's neck. Looked like an animal had ripped into his throat. She sits back on the floor and gives a giggle.

"I always wanted to do that, just like Lugosi," she says.[8]

I just stood there looking at her, scared out of my mind and shaking.

"Don't worry, I won't hurt you, Reuben,[9] *just sit down. Sick and tired of fools. Got no time for them anymore. Light my ciggy, while you're at it."*

"Name's not Reuben," I managed to get out.

She laughed.

"Ain't what I meant. Light my damn ciggy, or I'll tear your throat out."

I didn't even think about what I was seeing or doing. There she was, with a bullet hole in her chest, blood coming out all from it, and I stumbled around in the kitchen till I found the matches. I crouched down near her, my hands shaking, and she hands a cigarette out to me that she pulled out of a little, metal case, and I light it. She leans back, takes a breath of the smoke, and then puffs it out into the air, all relaxed. I'm just staring and she gives a cough with blood coming out onto her bottom lip. I look back at Vern's body with blood running down the neck, then at her, and she looks at me with the cigarette hanging out of the one side of her mouth.

"I feel bad for Dorothy, but she's better off this way. I did for her what I should have done years ago. That just leaves you and me doesn't it?" she asks, puffing out more smoke.

"What...what you gonna do?" I asked as I glanced at Vern real quick.

"Stop your damn shaking, you and me are all right. Guess you want me to tell you 'bout myself now," she says.

I sat down on mama's couch, looking at her. I'm sitting there, God forgive me. Right then I didn't even think one bit about Vern and his broken body just lying there between us. I couldn't think of a single word to say, because what was she? What was I looking at?

She took a bullet straight to the chest and she's talking now like it was some cough due to cold. I think that, and it's like she knew it and says what I needed to hear.

"I'm something else is what, ain't nothing to do with a cold. Well, I'm tired now, we'll talk tomorrow. You got a cellar, right? I don't remember where it is and I don't have the energy to dig it out of yah."

"You ain't never been here before."

She gives me this look like she was annoyed.

"Right. Let me say it again, you got a cellar, nice and dark too, remind me where it is. Do I get to it outside or..."

I pointed to the side where the hall was, the door to it was there.

"The cellar's down there. No lights, though, mama never got the electricity down there."

"Don't matter, better that way. Any light get down there?"

"Yeah, when the sun's up, a little comes in the windows."

"You got a way you can see?" she asks, standing up with her cigarette.

"Don't you need...a doctor, something?"

There she giggles again. I felt a chill run over me like she was laughing over my grave.

"Nah. Don't make me ask another time, you got a way you can see down there?"

"I can get a candle."

"Cellar's there, right?" she asks and points to the door.

I gave her a nod.

"You get a candle and follow me," she says, going into the dark.

I heard her shoes going down into the cellar while I found a candle. When I go down there, I can see near the bottom the glow from her cigarette. I get close and she's looking around like she can see without light, then she points at the old coal furnace.

"Think you can fit a body in there? Probably, eh?"

"You...Vern?" I asked and then mumbled something.

"Nah, not that chump, we'll deal with him tomorrow. In fact, I'll bring him down here before I get some rest. It's me what's going in there," she said, pointing at the furnace.

I stood there with the candle and she went back upstairs, so I followed. When I get up there, she goes to Vern's body and picks him right up without making a sound. It was like he was a pillow. I followed as she brought him down into the cellar and watched as she tossed him on the floor near the furnace. I don't know how I even stood there and watched it all. Without saying another word, she opens the door to the furnace and climbs on in there. Before she grabs the door to pull it shut, she looks at me and tosses the last bit of her cigarette on the dirt floor.

"You get some rest now and don't you dare lock me in here or try anything, or I'll make you look like him," she says and points at Vern.

I just nodded and watched as she went into the furnace and pulled the door shut, though she couldn't lock it from in there. I must have stood there for a while, because the candle melted down quite a bit. I could feel some of the wax on my hand. I didn't know what else to do. The Angel's in the furnace, Vern's body's just lying there with those marks on his neck, some of the skin and flesh ripped off, and his mouth open all frightful like a scream should be coming out. So I went up to my old room and somehow found the courage to try to sleep. I don't think I did at all and that ain't no surprise. I heard some sounds now and then, thought maybe I heard her cough through the vents once. Could have been her, I don't know. Parts of that night felt like eternity. Before I knew it, I could see the sun creeping up, and the light started to come in the window. I sat up and looked at it, thinking maybe it was all some sort of dream. I guess my mind wouldn't have it any other way, but it was that other way.

I went downstairs, and there she was, the Angel, sitting at our old table looking out the window with a cigarette hanging in her one *hand. She was leaning on her other hand, with one leg on the other kicking it playfully, and letting a thin puff of smoke out of her mouth.*

"Morning," she said.

She turned to me, putting the cigarette back in her mouth and taking it out smooth as a snake. There was soot and blood all over her. I noticed there was a lot of blood around her mouth that wasn't there when I left her in the cellar the last night. It looked like it had run all down her chin and down her neck. But the blood on her chest, from the bullet she took, well it was all gone, and it's like she knew I was staring at it. I hear her laugh and then she takes up her other hand and pulls open her shirt. I was going to turn my head because it was improper to see part of her there, but I had to look because of what I saw. Nothing there. No hole. No blood. Nothing.

"Yeah it's all gone. I told you it goes away quick once it's out of me. What you're seeing ain't my blood."

I just looked at her.

"Guess I need to talk now."

I didn't know what to think, just stood there as she put her shirt back in place.

"Ain't you gonna say something?"

"Want something to eat?" I said.

What a thing to say then, but it was all I could think of. She gave a little laugh.

"Nah, I...how did it go again in that old book about that old egg in the castle?[10] Ah, well, I haven't supped, because it's morning, so I'll just say no thanks, I already ate."[11]

I looked around and couldn't see anything was made, so I don't know quite what she meant by that.

"Don't ask me if I want no strawberry preserves neither," she says and smiles.

I sat down opposite her and just watched her. She eyed me funny, and it was so silent I figured I should say something.

"What's your name?"

"On with that again are yah? Your wife don't know nothing about me, huh?"

"No," I said.

She laughed.

"Ah, that's how it starts, that's how it starts," she said as she pointed her cigarette at me, "Most of the time anyway. A little flirt, a little smile, then there's some words, then there's more. Before too long any fool caught in it is too deep and weak to get out. But you're such a good boy goof you don't have to worry about me and your wife ain't got to worry neither. That's nice of yah. Call me Etta Kett."[12]

"You mean like the girl in the funnies?"

"Yeah, let's go with that one. You want me to make you something to eat, goof?"

"Yeah...yeah..." I said back to her, dumbly.

She puts the cigarette back in her mouth and gets up, walking over to mama's things like she lived there for years. I thought for a bit, and then I remembered the night before and how Vern's body was down in the cellar.

"What about his...Vern, what're we gonna do?"

The eggs were sizzling then, and she turns her head to me.

"Told yah, I took care of it."

"You didn't say nothing about it."

"Said I wasn't hungry and this ain't my own blood on me," she said with a mean smile and went back to cooking.

I still don't know if she meant what I thought she did. So I just stayed silent then after what I had seen. Soon, she brought over a plate with two eggs and a nice slice of ham like she was mama or something.

"I can cook, too, how about that? Perfect girl," she says to me, giving a short laugh, "Too bad ain't no one seen or understood it but you."

I just stare at the food, and she sits back down, putting the cigarette back in her mouth.

"My smoke bothering yah?"

"Nah. I just..."

"Don't like girls who smoke, I know. Forget it, go on and eat then."

So, I did, and it was a fine meal. Such an odd thought to be having among all that I saw the last night, but I ate it. At first I didn't feel hungry, I felt sick, but once I started to eat it's like I remembered I needed to and it was good.

"You like it?" she asks.

"Yeah, yeah, real good..."

"Don't you worry about Vern anymore. I told you I took care of it. Father Time had it coming to him.[13] *Men like that don't deserve nothing. I did that for Dorothy."*

I was scared of her, but I managed to say something. You'd have thought I would have before. Would have thought I would have tried to stop her or something but I didn't. But I said something right then.

"Vern was a good man. Knew him most of my life and he never did nothing to no one. Now I don't know what you thought he..."

That right there made her mad.

"What I thought? Thought?!" she screams standing up and staring at me with blazing eyes.

"I don't need to think!" she says, taking out the cigarette a second and pointing at me, "I don't need to think 'bout nothing. I can see it all," she says, moving her hands around, "I can see everything, you get that goof? You can't see evil in people like me because you're too damn good! You want the skinny on what that Vern did and why his Dorothy was crying that one time you heard well I'll tell yah! That what you want?"

I just shook my head.

"You fill in the damn details yourself! He had his chance to let it

go and live a good life but he came crawling back like the worm he was meant to be. He didn't have no brain, no will, couldn't even think for himself. Too stupid. He had what he needed and he gave it up then! He had it all! He had her! Like all them people listening to that preaching when we went on our little ole' walk. Good? Ha! You don't know nothing about them and you didn't know nothing about him. You know what he showed you. That's all. That don't mean nothing. Even when I drop some lines all them years ago about that Vern you still can't figure it out because you're too damn good. He showed you what he wanted you to see. They all do! He shows you, his family, all his friends, anyone, what he wants you to see. He ain't the only one. They're all like that. Wanted to do the mattress jig, so he got that. But he ain't worth nothing. Did that jig while he's got a wife who wonders why they don't have kids. Well I found out why. You just forget about him. His wife deserves better if she can find a lick of anything now."

I just couldn't believe what she was saying but all these little things I remembered and wondered about made sense right then. I still couldn't believe it in spite of that and just babbled the same thing that got her going before. I didn't even believe the words myself at that point.

"Vern was a good man."

She laughed and slapped the table hard then. Made my plate, and me, jump a tad.

"You think you know about him or any man?!" she yells at me, leaning forwards.

That scream had me scared. There was this power to it.

"Sorry, guy. You don't get it, how could you? I told you, you're too good for me."

There was that line again.

"You stop with your telling the dead they were better than they were, you get it? No one ever speaks ill of the dead, well they should sometimes, understand?"

I nodded, because as much as I hated to admit it, there was something about what she was saying.

"So let me tell it to you then, since you wanted to know for so long, then you'll know why I say that to you," she says, breathing out smoke.

I nodded.

"Remember when I told you I ain't no kid outside that church some years back?"

"Yeah, sure do."

"I ain't nothing. Don't know what I am myself. If you was to figure it, well I'd be around, hmm let's see...yeah about 93."

"Ain't no way. You look just like the last time I saw you, can't be older than 30."

She laughed then.

"Well, like any girl that makes me feel nice to know you see me so young. Makes me feel like someone still desires me. But I don't wrinkle, so I don't have to worry about it anyway."

"What?"

"Let me just tell all. I'll get it all out now. Then I need to be on my way and you can go do your thing now that you'll finally have what you wanted."

I looked at her and waited. She took that as my approval, then took another puff from her cigarette.

"Been around a long time... I was born before the war, but I should make it clear, I mean what some still call the War of Northern Aggression.[14] Not the Great War.[15] I lived not so far from here, Spotsylvania. Nice little farm. Peaceful life. I was a lucky girl, I thought. I found a good man who cared about me right after my parents died. Well, then that war happened. We weren't together that long, didn't have no kids yet, had no luck. You know you wouldn't think it would be so hard to have kids... For some people it is because of things they can't control, like that idiot Vern, but with

us it was just taking time. So, he, I mean Ezra, that was his name, goes off to that war. I was scared for us. Didn't want him to die.

"Oh, he didn't die like you might be thinking, he came back, dead in other ways. Wrote me letters, too, before he came home. Lots of letters. Each one was like another glass of busthead. After the Federals came through Fredericksburg, he got injured and came back home. I was elated. Wasn't dead. Injured, but not dead. Came back missing his left hand, but otherwise the man I remembered, and I loved him even more. We made love that first night, I can remember it now. Every part of me needed him. I gave him everything I had and fell asleep on his chest. One of the last happy moments I can remember..."

She took a puff of her cigarette then and looked out the window, putting her chin on her hand and thinking. It even looked like her eyes had a sadness in them. Then she starts again.

"Oh it was bliss then, I was so happy, hardly noticed he seemed distant at first, then it was obvious. He'd curse at me for nothing, would move away when I tried to kiss him. I knew something was wrong. I couldn't even put a hand on him sometimes without him pulling away and I was left there wondering if I did something. Made me feel real empty sometimes. Like I wasn't even there, like I was nothing. It's this rot that sticks to them when they're like that. Man, woman, it follows them like they're rotten. Guess they are. It was like he had died, in a way, that's what I meant before. Well, I found out why he was acting that way quick. During the war he got involved with hookers, couldn't quit it. Gave me some filth, the son of a bitch. I had never been with anyone else. The bastard had been around with some other girl, and then he ups and throws me out of the house, can you believe that? Told everyone I was fooling around on him," she said pointing at me strongly, "Couldn't find work, was getting sick, too broken to get any help, and it would have been worse if I did. The pain was horrible. He put that filth in me, body and soul,

and I'm living in the dirt. I watched what beauty I had left dying in front of me. You know what that's like, Reuben?"

"I don't know what you mean," I said.

"Eh, you men don't know nothing about it. Girls like yah the older you get. Not like that with us women. So, there I was, finished, tainted, cast out, and I wanted him dead. I wanted them both dead. But I was sick and dying. One night I was in Fredericksburg here, streets were still a mess from the war and the rain was thick.[16] *Broken buildings everywhere and there was me no better than them. Somehow found myself in the mud, just didn't want to get up anymore. Wanted to lay myself down and be dead like all those Southern boys at the Sunken Road.*[17] *I just laid face down breathing in muck. So I feel these hands picking me up and someone takes me out of the weather. Blacked out. When I came to, I found myself in this ramshackle little place and sitting across from me is this old negro woman. Boy was she skinny. I was all cleaned up by her. She smiles at me when I get up and asks if I'm hungry. By that point, I was so broken I just started to cry. Nice woman, she comforts me and asks me what's the matter and why I was out on the streets like that, all dirtied up, with no one. Treated me better than anyone before her I'd say. So I told her, I told her everything. I was keeping much of the secret then, but I let it all out, for her, because of what she did for me.*

"She sits there and listens to me, just staring. When I was finished, I cried. Oh, how I cried. Looking at my dress, stained from the mud and my sickly hands... Then that woman, who told me she was called Mama Hany, tells me I reminded her something of herself long ago. She looked about 60, but then she tells me this crazy thing, says she was almost 200. Said she came over on the slave ships long ago. Of course, there's no way I thought it possible, being how young she looked, for how old she said she was, but I was too gone then to hear what she was really saying. Then, she explains she was ripped from her home and brought here, she came with this man. Love of

her life. They helped each other and survived all that horror and then he did her wrong for another girl. When she started to talk about that part she got madder than I ever saw a woman get mad before. She went on about how they survived all that suffering together, they were linked like that, you know? She thought they were bonded, and then she says how she couldn't believe he'd give up everything they had and what they made it through together for something so fleeting. Well, after she calmed down she says to me, see honey, see how I was filled with the same kind of hate? Yeah, I says, and she says she did something about it. And then she sat there, saying nothing.

"So, I asked her what she did. She says she can tell me and give me the choice myself, but if I was looking for revenge, I'd have to do some horrible things to get there. I was in such a state it didn't matter to me and she could see it. I said I wanted him dead. I wanted to see him praying to the Lord before me and crying. I wanted him on his knees begging me for another day as I cut him open. And I said I wanted justice and I wanted people to know what real justice was. I wanted to show them. I wanted to do to him like he did to me but worse.

"So, she says to me she can help, just like some woman a long time ago helped her. She said I can have my beauty, never get old, never die, and never get sick. She said the sickness he gave me will come right out of me. But, she added, I will still feel pain of all kinds, it just won't ever kill me. She says I can do all that for you, little one, but that poison you got in you, you ain't gonna ever get it out. She opened her hands and said look at me, look what it made me. She said people ain't never gonna change. White men, negroes, anyone, all the same. They all do bad things, they ain't never gonna get better. She goes back to how old she is and she tells me this special secret she can give me. I can live forever, I can get my revenge, and there's no way he can stop me. But, it's going to cause me a lot of

pain, physical pain, and I'm going to feel it all. She said it's like having a child, but unlike that it's built on hate. After she got her revenge, the only reason she kept going on was because she wanted to see the world change. She told me she waited over 100 years to see if people would get any better. She waited to see how the world went and saw it was all the same, just looked different. She said to me again that poison never gonna leave your body and someday, like me, you'll be ready to quit it. But if you want to get your revenge and get that out of you, well, I can tell you how. But you have to do horrible things.

"I'll do anything, doesn't matter, I told her. She says to me, I don't mean to that man that done you wrong, I mean you have to do worse things. And you have to keep on doing those things if you want to keep going. Until, like me, you give it up, go through all the pain to be human again and then fade away like everyone else. If you stay on the path, you have to do worse. I said I didn't care, anything, anything to erase what he did, to erase what everyone did to me. I wanted everyone to feel the pain I did, I wanted to show the world what it was and crush it in my hand," she said as she acted like she was crushing a living thing in her fingers, "So Mama Hany tells me there's a way, a dark path. I won't bother you with all the particulars, Reuben, but she explained I needed to find a man and I had to get him to put his seed in me. But, she says, the child that comes from it can't have anything to do with love. You got to hate it. You have to hate everything about it, because it came from a man you hated. She says you have to let that baby run its course, but before it can be born, when you reach the seventh month, you got to do things worse than revenge. And she told me what to do, and she said when you make that fluid, from that horrible thing you do, you got to drink it. And when you drink it you can live forever, getting your revenge, dealing justice, just like you want. But it comes at a price, because the pain of living will still be with you and there's lots to learn. It

ain't like being human any more. She said, you'll learn tricks your-self, but I warn you, that poison ain't never gonna come out of you. But I didn't care. So, I did what she said.

"Now, I never experienced giving birth to a child, so I don't know about that, but I'd say the pain I went through must be worse. When I first found a man I hated, I made sure he was as nasty as could be. Was like Ezra, leaving his wife at home, with kids too. I felt bad for them, part of me, but I was so focused on my ends it didn't matter. Once I did that horrible thing and I drank that liquid she told me how to make, the pain I felt has to be something like dying. Something like giving birth and dying at the same time. Was so bad I tried to hang myself, but I wouldn't die. I felt all that pain, and getting myself down took a lot of trouble, but that wound on my neck healed, the bones healed too, and then the pain was gone, and I looked at myself, and it was like I was reborn. I looked like I did before he went off to war, like nothing had changed. All tight and nubile, just like a man likes. Couldn't believe it, so I tried it again, to kill myself. Tried it a couple of times. Once, I cut open my wrists and my throat. My God was it painful, but I came back from that. I think it was then that I noticed my blood wasn't the same anymore. It turns into this powder when it's out of me for a little bit, just blows away. So I tried other ways to kill myself to see if there was some-thing Mama Hany missed. Tried to hang myself again, but worse, and, ha, did that one take me time to get out of. It was like I was remaking my body again and again. Anything that happened to me I could erase and start all over. Why, reminds me, I never tried it, but I bet yah if I'd be chopped up to pieces it would all come back together somehow. Once I saw what she taught me was true, I went to do what I set out to do.

"I came to the farm at night so no one would see me. It was raining and it felt wonderful. I didn't care about the cold, didn't mean anything anymore. I just felt that cold water dripping over me

as I walked. Felt like that was my new world, like I was part of the rain. Wasn't sure how I was going to kill the vermin, but I went and saw Ezra and that chunk of lead still doing their thing.[18] *They didn't see me when I looked in the one window. They were sitting there eating dinner and there's this big knife he used for skinning sitting on the table, so I eyed that up. I look at him a bit again and it makes me sick he seems to be sittin' there all fine with that sickness in him, if it's still there and she didn't get it? Some justice, I thought, so I'm gonna make my own. I come around, check the door. Locked. So I knock loud and I hear this talking in there and then the door opens and there's the swine staring at me. His eyes get real big like some animal and I push past him before he can think, grabbing that knife right off the table. Next thing I know, he's at my back grabbing me and trying to get it out of my hands and the girl's screaming. Well, he was still stronger than me or, well...I wasn't yet used to what I am, and he throws me down, then picks up his pistol and shoots me without even thinking about it. What a sting! Close to where that other clown shot me right here,"* she says, moving her shirt some and showing me where there should have been a hole from the last night.

I was about to look away for a second.

"What? You don't want to see what I got to offer?" she asks with a soft giggle, *"Don't matter, you won't do anything with it anyway. I know you're too good."*

She paused there until I was looking at her again and gave a little smile.

"So, after that bullet I was on the ground gasping, and there's blood coming out of my mouth, but then I pull myself up. I look at him, smiling, all that blood coming down my chin. Knife was on the ground, so I pick it up while he's gawking and step forwards. He shoots me again, this time in the head. I hear the girl give another scream and she's frantic, saying God knows what. My ears were ringing and it felt like a train had hit me in the skull. So they're

fighting about my body and I'm listening to them argue, and with everything, I just started to laugh. Then there's this silence and just me laughing there on the floor with blood all over myself. I grab that knife and pull myself up again, though my body was wracked with pain. I felt every bit of it, just like Mama Hany said. But I couldn't die.

"He was just staring at me, shaking. No idea what I looked like, but it must have been lovely. I took that knife and I went for him, sticking him like a hog. You should have heard the sound he made, ha! Sounded like a little baby giving a cry. Isn't that how it is with some of them? They act all strong but there's a child inside. I made sure he was still alive, and then I told him I was going make him watch everything I did to the girl. I did things to her that would make Satan toss me from Hell. Then I finished with him. Even when he was nothing but a shell I kept doing things to what was left until, well, until like that Vern it was all gone or nothing you could even call part of a man. Even killed the animals on the farm, every last one of them. I ripped the pigs to pieces. I crushed the chickens' skulls," she said with this sinister look in her eyes, "Yeah and all the cattle. They sure have a lot of blood. You ever hear a cow scream?" she asked while looking at me.

All I could do was shake my head.

"Yeah, well I reveled in that sound thinking of what he did to me, I killed all of them. I remember the look in the one's eyes as I tore at it. Didn't matter what it was, the state I was in. I wanted all those memories dead. I was covered in red and then I burned it all down, anything that reminded me of him. As the farm burned, I sat high up in a tree in the woods across the field, watching people scrambling to do something about it. Part of me felt bad about that, for a brief moment, until I realized all of them, all those liars, they were on his side when he tossed me aside. So there I perched, smiling. See that's because it felt good. Felt better than I thought. I thought I would

have been empty, you hear that about revenge that when you do it you feel less than before. But I didn't, I felt great, better than I had in a long time. But, Mama Hany was right that the poison doesn't go away. That pain that made me comes back and I need the liquid to keep doing what I'm doing. Had to figure things out like she said. Figured it out that sleeping in dark places, like your coal furnace, makes me heal up faster. Learned how to read people, too, by staring in their heads. Sometimes only bits come through, sometimes parts of it are wrong," she said, pausing to look outside, "But, unlike her, I'm not waiting for people to change, I know there's good out there, but most of the world ain't, most of them out there are just as crooked as they were back when I gave up being human.

"So, that's what I do. I get my revenge year after year. It's easy, too, so many men out there have no sense of right. They do what they want, damn their wife, damn their kids, if they have 'em, their family, friends, they just ain't got no sense of goodness when it comes down to it. They go into their church, they give their money, they talk those words about gates and paths, but they ain't worth nothing. They just thinkin' about what they want and they go for it. Don't care nothing about what could come later. I'd call them selfish but after it's all done the trouble they find themselves in ain't nothing a selfish person would want. And they easy, too. So, now and then, when I need it, I choose another one to break and I dig in his brain to make sure he's good for it. When he gives me his seed, I'm through, leave him to his rewards or, like that Vern you thought was a good man, give him what he deserves. So, that's it, that's all there is to it. I go on, year after year, unchanging thing that I am, and I give the world what it needs. Like some angel fallen from heaven who gave up on God."

When she said that my blood went cold, because I remembered that's how I once thought of her, like an angel in a play I once saw. But then she said worse things after taking another puff from her cigarette, as she stood up near the little window above mama's old sink

"That stew, that liquid, doesn't last long, though, spoils. If I don't have any for more than a month, I start to feel that pain like birthing and dying, so I had to find a way to keep it going longer, a way to make it easier so I had to bother with less fools. Found a way to make it stay in the body longer. Just have to put a little in some tobacco and dry it."

Then she takes her cigarette out of her mouth and raises it in front of her face, smiling at it. She looks at me without saying a word, then puts it back in her mouth, breathes in real deep, and then puffs the smoke out into the air. I wanted to run, then, but was too scared of her.

"I'll save you from breathing it now, this one did its work," she said, putting it out on her hand without a wince like she was used to it.

So she takes the cigarette in her palm, and looks around.

"You mind if I take your mama's clothing, some of it? Need to get this stuff off of me, all covered in blood. Get myself cleaned up a bit, too."

"Yeah...yeah there's some things upstairs. Bathroom is, mama had the plumbing put in just um...uh...you..."

"You just stay put here, Reuben."

I hear her going upstairs to mama's room and she starts looking around. Would have thought it was mama herself if I didn't know it was her, or some ghost that hadn't quit the Earth. Heard her get in the bath and clean up. When she came down, she was all naked walking towards me with her hair still a little wet. I froze, I thought she wanted it to be me next, but she just holds out the bloodied clothes towards me in front of my chest.

"There take those."

I couldn't move, so she just smiled and dropped them on the floor in *front me. Then she goes and looks in mama's old mirror in the living room and starts to dress. I never saw such a creature like that. She was beautiful. I hope you don't mind my saying that. Not like you, I mean, she was beautiful in this different way. Something like an angel, but not. Something older. Something with a purpose more than little old you or me could ever figure. She put mama's clothes on and then comes over to me. She was counting some money in her hands she must have had in her other clothes. I noticed then that where she burned her hand with the cigarette looked like nothing had happened to it, it had healed right up. Mama's clothes didn't fit her quite right, but she looked about as normal as any other woman I guess. Maybe just a bit out of her time.*

"I'm gonna get going now. You take those clothes I put there and you stuff them in the furnace downstairs. I put Vern's clothes in there already. Burn it all, that way no one knows nothing about him. Might want to clean your floor over there too," she says, pointing to some blood I hadn't noticed before, "His wife's better off not knowing anything about last night. Best she remember him otherwise, since you know her and all. I saw it in her eyes long time ago, she doesn't need to feel any more of it. I'll let her die believing the lies I'm sure he told her so she can go on with a bit of dignity. I'll do that for you. Now come over here, goof."

I was thinking it was me who was next, so I stood still. She walks right over to me, grabs my shirt, and brings my head down in front of hers. She stares at me then, real deep, and I felt that flapping inside my skull for a moment, then it was gone.

"I told you to cool off. Nothing you need to worry about. You see me all in my birth clothes and you still don't do nothing. You stop worrying. I told you, you're just too good for me, and you keep it that way, you get me?"

She puts a kiss right on my lips, pats my head, and starts walking for the door.

"I need to see a man about a dog," she says, and walks right out.[19]

Well, I couldn't have it end at that, so I went out after her, and there she was walking from the sidewalk into the road, sun shining on her. She looked like something sent from Heaven then, strange as it is to say.

"What you want now?" she asks, smiling at me.

"Where're you going, where'll you go?"

"Oh, I don't know, probably back to a big city, maybe Washington. Depends where the weather takes me. Now you listen here, one more time. You forget about me. You go back to your wife and kids. You go back there and you live your nice, honest life, Middy Grove. You live that life of love where you keep things honest. You go back and keep them happy till they, or you, are gone. You make sure you teach them kids of yours to do the right things, so they can be one of the good ones, I know you can. Bye now," she said, and turned to walk away down to the train station, I figured.[20]

I watched her walk away, and not once did she turn back. When I went back into the house and got myself together, I took her clothes down into the cellar, stuffing them in the furnace. Vern's clothes were right in there, just like she told me. Couldn't find nothing else of him, nothing at all. Thought maybe she buried him in the floor, but the dirt hadn't been touched anywhere, and the shovel was sitting in the same place it was the night before. I looked a bit to be sure, dug around here and there, but there was nothing. Ground hadn't been touched since probably the cellar was dug years ago. I'm not sure if what she meant about the blood on her and eating was true, but I don't want to think about it. That was the last I saw of her, but she's always been on my mind. Not for the reasons you may have thought when you started to read this. I never wanted you to know. I hope you can understand why, when you read it all here hon. I loved you and the kids dearly, never did anything wrong to any of you. Never would. Now and then, when you asked what was bothering me, now you know. I don't know what to think of it myself, but I'll say this. You make sure you tell our kids again and again, and their kids, that there's bad people out there in the world. Some of them are down-right evil. Some are worse than that. There's some bad people out there that can make a girl want to turn into a thing like her.

I'll be waiting for you up there, where the good ones are, my real Angel.

- Love you Dearly,
Your Middy

Historical Notes

Middy Grove's Letter to His Sister

1. The picture shows the actual pickle factory, as it stood around 1927. The building that housed the factory had been in place since 1849 and has been used for a variety of purposes since construction.
2. This was one of two most typical words used at this time for African American that was not a racial slur. It was not common to capitalize it outside of titles, such as for books, until later.
3. Middy is here referencing an actual event, reported in "The Free Lance" from its January 1st issue in 1921. The article's headline is "ATTEMPTED ROBBERY Two Marines Tried to Enter Goldsmith's Clothing Store in Dead of Night." In the article, it states exactly: "Following a robbery by an [word illegible] negro [sic] on Xmas Eve night when he grabbed her pocketbook and escaped..."
4. Goldsmith & Son was a large, Jewish-owned clothing store in Fredericksburg. The original owner was Benjamin Goldsmith, and his sons were Jacob and Joseph. Joseph partnered with his father to manage the store in 1902. Goldsmith died in April of 1920 and his sons worked the store until the 1950s when the building was eventually demolished. It used to stand at what is 920 Caroline Street. Mr. Goldsmith, upon his death, was said to be the oldest citizen of Fredericksburg and was a prominent businessman because of his store, the oldest one in the city, and one of the most recognized in the state of Virginia at the time.
5. This story is taken from the same article reference in the previous note. The Marines were in uniform, attempted to rob the store around 1:30AM, broke the window with a pipe, and as Middy mentions, a Mrs. E. H. Backley called the police, but had to use a neighbor's phone since she did not own one. The Marines later were arrested at a "Greek café."
6. This street has been renamed in Fredericksburg a few times throughout the city's history. Today it is called Caroline Street. In the 1920s the title of "Main" was used because it was thought it made the city sound more modern.
7. The building that originally housed Bond's Drug Store, which read "Drugs and Seeds" on the front, still stands today, and has been through numerous hands.
8. Middy is here talking about the "State Normal and Industrial School for Women in Fredericksburg," founded in 1908, later renamed the State

Teachers College (also known as the Fredericksburg Teachers College) in 1924. In 1938 it was renamed "Mary Washington College." In Middy's day the school was primarily for women. Today it is known as the University of Mary Washington.

9. Four people are listed with the name "Vernon" in the city directory of 1921, including a "Vernon Kendall" who lived at 401 Water Street. The author merely used the name for historical relevance for the character.

10. A line of the lyrics from the actual song "The Vamp," written by Byron Gay and published in 1919. "Vamp" was a popular slang term for a young girl who would deceive men. It was rarely used to refer to deceitful men. More information is present in the historical essay, including a discussion of this song.

11. The classic flapper hairstyle was referred to typically as "bobbed" at this time, though it is simply a common shoulder-length cut today. This style caused some controversy in the 1920s. The description of her clothing that follows is based on photographs of young girls (Comment: "young women"?) from the time.

A Letter from Dorothy Kendall to Her Sister Alma Tackett

1. Dorothy is discussing the Liberty Café, which, at the time, was across the street from the train station in Fredericksburg.

2. By 1920, the term flapper was seeing wider usage in the United States. Technically the term's origins come primarily from the late 19th Century, but in 1920 in particular, the silent comedy *The Flapper* made the term far more common in colloquial speech.

Middy Grove's Letter to His Sister

1. Middy here describes the essentials of this stage adaptation of a 1904 novel by Gene Stratton-Porter (1863 – 1924) of the same name. Forgotten today, the novel was extremely popular upon publication and was made into films, such as a successful production from 1928, and plays.

2. Originally located at 1006 Caroline Street, the famous Opera House was built in 1883 and was a popular entertainment spot in the city for plays, and then films. It was removed in 1956 to build Woolworth's, a department store, which currently stands as an antique store.

3. In the original novel this character is called the "Swamp Angel," and the book's meaning is actually that only a person of high birth can do good things, not an orphan, unless they were actually high-born. The play referred to this character, however, as "The Angel." Middy gives a brief

description of the actual stage design for this play as it appeared at the Opera House.

4. Highway 1 would come near Fredericksburg in 1925 and was a big event for the city, partially because many of their roads were antiquated and needed modernized, as well as the lighting. It was seen by many citizens as a step towards the future.

5. At the time Frederickssburg featured few street lights that were electric, except for large, domed lights hanging over important intersections. Otherwise, the streets would be almost completely dark at night.

6. Located at 209 Fauquier Street, this was a popular roadhouse at the time, but it is now a privately owned home.

7. Though this slang is outdated, its meaning should be clear. The reader should note that this character speaks in flapper slang many times, and words that require translation will be noted further in the notes.

8. This information was taken from an actual weather report in 1921.

Middy Grove's Letter to His Sister

1. Fredericksburg United Methodist Church, which was built in the early 19th Century, still stands at 308 Hanover Street. The Reverend H. L. Hout was the head of the church at the time, and gave sermons every evening the week of this letter in 1921.

2. This would be translated today as "you having a crush on me."

3. This is an extremely quick reference to two examples in old vampire literature of a vampire having a strong grip. One from the 1854 short story "The Mysterious Stranger," an unauthorized English translation of the German "Der Fremde" (1844), elements of which were later reused by Bram Stoker in his novel *Dracula*.

4. This would be translated today as "get lost" or "get out of my face."

The Free-Lance

1. Known affectionately at the time as the "Skyscraper," this was the tallest building in Fredericksburg until a fire in 1963, which was caused by a coffee urn. The building housed a bank and even a gym at one point. It was at the corner of Princess Anne and William Street (then called Commerce Street).

2. This was a popular day-trip destination for residents of Fredericksburg, who would take buses to the location. The beach, now part of King George County, is privately owned currently, and all of the original beach houses and attractions are gone.

The Death of Mrs. Thomas C. Grove

1. At the time it was typical for deceased, married women to be referred to by their husbands' name. This obituary is based on similar obituaries from The Free-Lance at the time.
2. The Fredericksburg City Cemetery still exists and includes many old graves. The Gothic gate has fallen into disrepair but there are private donors working to repair it.

Letter written in 1928, by Middy Grove

1. This detail is historically accurate.
2. Middy is referring to St. George's Episcopal Church, which still stands in Fredericksburg at 905 Princess Anne Street. Around 1925 the original gas lamp, no longer functioning, was still outside of the church.
3. This term was also one of endearment at the time like "sweetie."
4. The Princess Anne Hotel was a famous location in Fredericksburg for many years. One of its most famous visitors was Winston Churchill. It ceased to be a hotel and was sold off in 1977, and today is an office building. Much of the original structure is there, but the rooms and lobby were converted over time, making it difficult to discern the original shape of the space. Old photographs not in the public domain, however, provide such details.
5. This is a reference to the role the silent actress Theda Bara played as "The Vamp" in *A Fool There Was* (1915). In one scene, one of her former lovers threatens her with a pistol, but she laughs and taps down the barrel with a flower.
6. The hospital in Fredericksburg at this time was called Mary Washington. The original building was opened in 1899 and had only eight rooms, but by the 1920s was much larger, as an addition and second-story had been added by 1910. In 1928 it was significantly increased to a total of 75 beds. African Americans were only permitted, in most cases, to be in the "colored" section of the hospital during this time.
7. It was tradition into at least the 1950s in many American families to have the funeral at home before burial, not at a funeral home. The living room or parlor was the typical place for the corpse.
8. She is making a reference to Bela Lugosi, who famously played Count Dracula on stage in the late 1920s. He had yet to appear in a film as the character based on the time of the action presented here. The Universal adaptation would not appear until Valentine's Day of 1931. Technically, even in the film, there is never any graphic biting. In fact, Bela Lugosi never reveals two extended canines because the prosthetic technology

did not yet exist. So she be referring to the general idea of it and the stage version specifically.

9. She is not mistaken here and stating Middy's name incorrectly. "Reuben" was a term used in the flapper era for someone who was uneducated and usually from the country.

10. She means "rich person" here.

11. She's making reference to a famous line in the novel *Dracula* where the Count implies he drank blood or feasted on a human being when he says "...I have dined already, and do not sup" (Chapter II).

12. Etta Kett was an extremely popular comic strip character that had her heyday in the 1920s and 1930s.

13. Here, she means in slang that Vern was a man over the age of 30, generally. Of course, in this context it has a dual meaning.

14. This used to be a way many Southerners referred to the American Civil War. At the time of the publication of this book there are even some older citizens in the South who still refer to the Union Army as the "Federals."

15. Since World War II had yet to happen she means World War I.

16. Fredericksburg was devastated during the Battle of Fredericksburg from December 11th to 15th in 1862. Much of the city was destroyed and looted, and, by the 1920s, it was still rebuilding due to a lack of government assistance. Many of the streets were still dirt and the poor, of all backgrounds, lived on side streets. African Americans were generally segregated to one area of the city, but they did live on other streets.

17. The "Sunken Road" originally referred to a section of Fredericksburg that is today controlled by the National Park Service. At the spot is a famous stone wall Confederate soldiers used to defend themselves successfully against the Union Army, which was never able to get within more than fifty yards. A famous photograph taken after the battle shows a variety of corpses lying against the wall along the road, to which "Etta Kett" is referring.

18. She means here the other woman her husband is with, who he left her for earlier in her story.

19. Her statement means she needs to get going, but in this context it can have a dual meaning, such as potentially suggesting she is involved in an affair, or in the case of this story perhaps is already working on another victim she is preparing to seduce.

20. The current train station is still in the location on 200 Lafayette Boulevard, where it would have been in the 1920s. Today the main terminal is a restaurant called "The Alpine Chef," but the station is still served by Amtrak and passenger trains can be taken from the city.

The Path of the "Vamp"

An Essay by Stanley Stepanic

I am currently an Assistant Professor at the University of Virginia who teaches an ever-popular course on vampires, which goes by the simple name of "Dracula." Dracula covers the origins of the vampire in pre-Christian Slavic belief and tracks its development into a symbol of human experience in the modern era. Students learn about nearly everything you could connect with a vampire such as disease, gender identity, and racial identity, among many other topics. One lecture every semester includes a brief discussion of the entity called the "vamp."

This particular novella in the reader's hands was a random thought that eventually came to life as something greater. For some time I was working feverishly on an epic-length sci-fi romance that takes place primarily in Fredericksburg, Virginia in the 1920s. Due to the amount of research and familiarity I developed with the location from visiting it in its modern state and reading through newspapers and archival information related to the time period, I decided to place a shorter work within the same setting. Thinking on the Golden Age of monsters in cinema, some alteration of *Dracula* (1931), seemed appropriate. I chose the vamp image that became a cultural revolution in the 1910s through the 1920s as a starting point due to my familiarity with the theme and its rather easy placement within the Roaring Twenties as part of the flapper tradition. One stipulation I put before myself was to complete any research on the vamp in "the raw," meaning without utilizing any previous scholarship.

As I tend to find in the field of vampire studies, ideas are often repeated without any proper fact-checking. This led, from the early 1960s into the modern day, into a proliferation of falsities surrounding vampires and vampire-related topics. Ideas such as the claim that Bram Stoker (1847 – 1912) invented the word "undead", that the hair on Count Dracula's palms was a superstition in the Victorian era concerning masturbation, or that the Vampire of Düsseldorf (Peter Kürten, 1883 – 1931) asked if he could hear his own blood spurting from his neck when he was executed by decapitation, are myths, though they can be found in a variety of reputable publications. Thus, the reader should note that research presented here is from the author's own delving into the history of the vamp *directly*, relying on primary texts from the time in question, and not modern-day interpretations or scholarship.

Though there are certainly attempts by other scholars to track the vamp, and a number of publications to prove this, the idea was to perform this writing cold in order to further discover the origins of the history that led to the story in this very book. Therefore, I refrained from consulting any texts or articles primarily published prior to 1929. So, to now begin, as I lead you through the history, what is the vamp?

"Her head fell back, but she wrapped her arms around me as if to hold me back." A watercolor from 1904 by Eugène Decisy (1866 – 1936) based upon the work of Paul Albert Laurens (1870 – 1934).

The image as it came to be known was not originally one of a supernatural quality, though it was connected to earlier examples in literature, transformed into an allegory. In simplest terms, it is a form of character known in literature from some of its earliest periods under the broad title of "femme fatale" (the fatal woman). The idea is simple and generally consistent; a young, beautiful girl, who uses her intelligence, but especially her sexuality, to lure men astray and bring them to ruin. The time period does not matter, nor does the setting. Her victims are often mature men established in life, typically depicted in a state of uncertainty concerning their waning vitality; easy prey for an astute predator. Various arguments have been made for characters in literature that generally fit these criteria of the femme fatale, including Lilith, or as was popular during the period of Decadence (starting in France in the 1870s), "Salome," daughter of Herod II in the New Testament who, though in the text unnamed, requests the head of John the Baptist after dancing for Herod Antipas, who said, "Ask me for anything you want, and I'll give it to you" (Mark 6:22).

Though perhaps something of a connection to the image, the idea of the femme fatale was not a concept actively discussed until the late 19th Century, though one can find earlier references, but soon became a classic trope that could be thought of as a female equivalent of the "Byronic Hero" character type of the same era. Earlier discussions from the end of the 18th Century are primarily French and it was not until the 1890s that the idea of a woman of lascivious qualities was more commonplace due to changing opinions on femininity stemming from what is often called today "first-wave feminism," or more properly the "New Woman" as it was known at the time. An issue of *The Cosmopolitan* from 1895, for example, discussed various women from Paris, including a singer who, the article stated, "sings the songs of the outer boulevards, that harsh song of the rabble, with a vigorous spirit that her physique of a femme fatale renders astonishingly effective." Similar phraseology through the 19th Century is quite simple to locate utilizing digital archives.

By the 1910s the concept of the femme fatale was generally understood in these terms, though by the middle of the decade at the latest it was known popularly as the "vamp" due to a very simple, and also complex, set of circumstances. Fin de siècle ("end of the century") culture produced a number of decadent works of art leading into the 20th Century from the macabre sexuality of Félicien Rops (1833 – 1898) to the Pre-Raphaelite Gothic resurrection fashioned by artists such as Sir Edward Coley Burne-Jones (1833 – 1898). Burne-Jones' son, Sir

Philip William Burne-Jones (1861 – 1926), a skilled painter is his own right, would never achieve the same level of fame as his father, though he did manage one important work that still resonates in the modern era, a painting first presented publicly on the 24th of April in 1897, slightly over a month before Bram Stoker's novel *Dracula* was first published, which was May 26th of that year. The painting was a simple composition titled "The Vampire," which you can see in the next image.

Phillip Burne-Jones "The Vampire" from 1897.

Philip Burne-Jones' only recognized work today, and sadly which only survives in black-and-white reproductions as well as at least one colorized version, the painting depicts a woman with long, dark hair gloating over the body of a man upon whom she partially leans, her arms extended to hold her upper body over him, her hair draping upon his stomach, and a sadistic smile just beginning to form on her face. Closer inspection reveals what appears to be the suggestion of a bite mark on the man's chest at the location of his heart, an idea perhaps influenced by Joseph Sheridan Le Fanu's (1814 – 1873) character "Carmilla," the titular vampire from the novella *Carmilla* (first serialized in 1871 and 1872) who bit her female victims on the breast. There is no verified connection, but Burne-Jones likely knew of the work in some fashion. The "vampire" in the painting as he titled her was supposedly modeled after Beatrice Rose Stella Cornwallis-West (née Tanner, 1865 – 1940), a once famous stage actress known more popularly as "Mrs. Patrick Campbell," though further evidence suggests it was actually another woman entirely used for the painting; an unknown model from Brussels.

Critics at the time suggested many things, including a possible connection to the short story by Théophile Gautier (Pierre Jules Théophile Gautier, 1811 – 1872) entitled "La Morte amoureuse" ("The Dead Woman in Love"), known under a variety of names such as "Clarimonde," though Burne-Jones himself seems to have never mentioned this possible connection (the first image of this essay is a watercolor from the story). Regardless, "The Vampire" was viewed as Burne-Jones' only work of significance at the time, though a critic in the *New York Times*, as reported in Volume XXXII (1902) of *Public Opinion*, stated that "it is exceedingly unfortunate that so much pother has been raised in the papers about Sir Philip and his 'Vampire.'" As is usually the reality of criticism in the arts, if the public shows interest, no breadth of negative words will matter. For, as time showed, interest in the mysterious vampire woman remained, and this led to a cultural revolution in a variety of media.

Upon the painting's first appearance in public, Burne-Jone's cousin, Joseph Rudyard Kipling (known in most publications simply as Rudyard Kiping, 1865 – 1936), penned a poem based on the image and the idea of the femme fatale called "The Vampire". The poem, now public domain, is presented in full below.

A fool there was and he made his prayer
(Even as you or I!)
To a rag and a bone and a hank of hair,
(We called her the woman who did not care),
But the fool he called her his lady fair—
(Even as you or I!)

Oh, the years we waste and the tears we waste,
And the work of our head and hand
Belong to the woman who did not know
(And now we know that she never could know)
And did not understand!

A fool there was and his goods he spent,
(Even as you or I!)
Honour and faith and a sure intent
(And it wasn't the least what the lady meant),
But a fool must follow his natural bent
(Even as you or I!)

Oh, the toil we lost and the spoil we lost
And the excellent things we planned
Belong to the woman who didn't know why
(And now we know that she never knew why)

And did not understand!

The fool was stripped to his foolish hide,
(Even as you or I!)
Which she might have seen when she threw him
aside—
(But it isn't on record the lady tried)
So some of him lived but the most of him died—
(Even as you or I!)

And it isn't the shame and it isn't the blame
That stings like a white-hot brand—
It's coming to know that she never knew why
(Seeing, at last, she could never know why)
And never could understand!

Kipling would not officially publish his poem until 1919 at the latest, though it was reprinted several times without his permission from the first presentation of Sir Philip's painting to the end of the 1910s. The original painting and the poem created a modern form of femme fatale for the era, one that largely retained its previous roots of a woman of ruin, yet which became more dominant in how she approached her victims, connected to changing opinions on women in media stemming from the "New Woman" and "Gibson Girl" images of the era, retitled "the vampire" or "vamp" for short. In this era of newfound women's liberation, stemming from a push for voting rights, more open female sexuality, and events such as the "Triangle Shirtwaist Factory Fire" of 1911, the vamp was a symbol both of women asserting their power and fears of the retribution of the patriarchal system they were overturning.

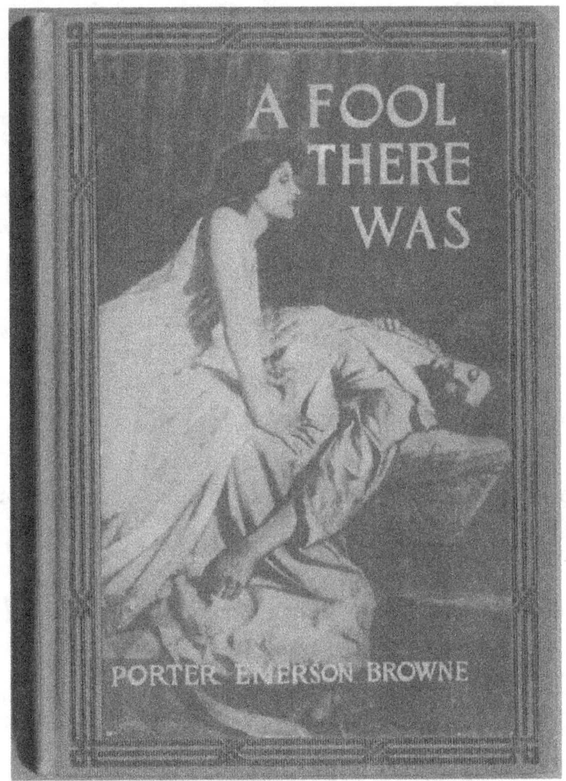

Cover of *A Fool There Was* by Porter Emerson Browne.

Though there are some film appearances of characters that could be consider early forms of the vamp or prototypes, in a way, the critical point for this transformation from whispers in literature, to painting, and then popular culture as a whole, was the film *A Fool There Was* (1915), based on a novel by Porter Emerson Browne (1879 – 1934) by the same name first published in 1909 and connected to a stage version, also of the same title and year, both inspired by the same painting and poem discussed earlier. The painting, in fact, appeared on the cover of the original, cloth-bound first edition of the novel, flipped horizontally, as shown in the previous image. For the play, the "Vampire" was depicted by Katherine Kaelred (also spelled as Katharine, 1882 – 1942), an Australian actress who immigrated to the United States in the same year she appeared as the character on stage. The next image presents a photograph, taken around this time, that appears to have been a promotional photo for *A Fool There Was*. The dress she wears and her hair style are similar to that of which she was shown in in Volume X of *The Theatre* in an article for the play entitled "A Vampire Woman at Close Range."

"Is she at all like the part she plays?" asked the journalist learning about Kaelred's performance.

A guide responded with, "She is. That is, she is quite capable of being irresistible. A man is much safer if he stays away from her. You will see."

The journalist then goes on to state, shortly after: "Her eyes are big and black, with the velvety brilliance our dreams give to the eyes of Cleopatra, one of the earliest vampires of history."

The basic idea of the story from the novel and play follows the character "John Schuyler" (known also as "Jack"), a diplomat who marries the woman of his dreams, who is a girl known since childhood, to create the ideal family. Browne's prose is extremely melodramatic, sometimes awkwardly so, with moments that feel overly theatrical. The Vampire (the character's name is capitalized in the novel), is given a past before the primary story begins, presented as an illegitimate daughter born into poverty whose mother dies of an uncertain illness. As she grows older, she becomes more beautiful, bathing nude in a nearby stream, and when her father returns to the poor hut in which she lives she kills him by merely walking towards him with an exaggerated gait until he strangely falls backwards over a cliff. The old woman who she lives with, and who raised her from an infant after her mother's death, simply replies "Bien" ("Good"). Her past thus set,

Katherine Kaelred Seated on Bench. Bain News Service photograph collection.

though not entirely explained, the young woman eventually finds her way onto the ship Schulyer is set to sail upon for a diplomatic mission in England.

His friend "Thomas Blake" soon meets the girl after he learned of a young man committing suicide because of a wanton woman, suspecting the strange woman who catches his friend's attention is likely one and the same. Unfortunately, he has no way of saving his friend from his fate, and Schuyler, soon involved in an affair, ruins his career, loses his family, and descends into drunkenness, his life left in ruins by the Vampire even when he is provided an opportunity to reconcile with his wife and rejoin her and their daughter. In spite of the awkwardness of the plot development, Browne's Vampire acts different than her predecessors. Her movements with flowers are symbolic and her appearances, coinciding with moments when Schuyler is more lucid, almost uncanny in their ability to capture the abusive manipulation tactics of a narcissist.

Alice Eis performs the "vampire dance" at the end of *The Vampire* (1913).

The popularity of this novel and play after release led to the first film vamp in 1910, the now lost short *The Vampire*, produced by Selig Polyscope Company (1896 – 1918 for film production). Running at 1000 feet in length, a standard used at the time to indicate for potential viewers the literal length of the film, which in this case would lead to roughly 10 minutes of viewing, it starred Margarita Fisher (née Fischer, 1886 –1975) and was based on Kipling's poem primarily, even including some of its lines as intertitles. Following this sadly lost film came yet another adaptation of Kipling's work, *The Vampire* (1913), starring Alice Hollister (Rosalie Alice Amélie Berger, 1886 – 1973), which according to sources followed a similar plot development yet the broken man in question reclaims his love and finds happiness in the end, changing the original story from one of tragedy to one of rediscovery. Hollister was so popular in the role that she reprised it, or similar characters, in three other films: *The Vampire's Trail* (1914), *The Siren's Reign* (1915), and *The Lotus Woman* (1916). Though she was referred to as "the original vampire" (*Photoplay*, June 1916) by the time she appeared in *The Lotus Woman*, her fame was quickly overshadowed, unfortunately, and none of her films with vamp characters have survived beyond publicity photos and stills.

Worldwide this phenomenon of manipulative women can also be found, for example, in roles such as that of "Mary" (Мэри) played by prima ballerina Elena Smirovna (Elena Aleksandrovna Smirnova, Елена Александровна Смирнова, 1888 – 1934) in *Child of the Big City* (*Дитя большого города*, 1914), but such examples should be considered reflective of the cultural climates of the time in their home countries, and not necessarily connected to the vamp tradition that began in the United States. Some scholars have mentioned other films, such as the French serial *Les Vampires* (1915 – 1916), which feature characters that could be considered prototypes or pseudo-vamps, but it is a crime serial in essence and does not, properly speaking, show the type of character the author is here discussing. Therefore, the 1910 and 1913 productions were the most important for the vamp's development as a character type. The standards set by these two films were continuations of the fame of Burne-Jones' painting, Kipling's poem, and Browne's subsequent adaptations in literature and theater, but it was a 1915 production which would solidify the image of the vamp for audiences, especially in the United States, becoming the true standard of the idea that would inspire manipulative female characters in media into the modern era.

An original movie poster for *A Fool There Was* (1915), created by Arthur Dickson (Fox Film Corporation).

A Fool There Was (1915) starred the once legendary Theda Bara (Theodosia Burr Goodman, 1885 – 1955), an actress who needs little introduction and whose biography is well-known. Sadly only a few examples of her work remain, including recently restored shots from *Salome* (1918, most likely censor cuts), first discovered in the mid-1990s in Spain and later verified and digitized for viewing, but *A Fool There Was* is fortunately complete and arguably her most culturally significant film in terms of its lasting effects. Bara's impact outside of this one example was immense for the short time she remained popular. Born in Cincinnati, Ohio to a Jewish family, she had dreams of acting after completing high school, finding her break in a minor role in the rediscovered film *The Stain* (1914), where she briefly appears as a nun, barely recognizable to even the most discerning viewer. In spite of playing a simple extra in this particular role, director Frank Powell (Francis William Powell, born 1877, date of death still unknown) was pleased with Bara's abilities and chose her to star as the central femme fatale character, the Vampire, of *A Fool There Was*. Not the first version of the plot by any means, as the reader is already aware, it was this film that would quickly catapult Bara and the vamp to widespread notoriety.

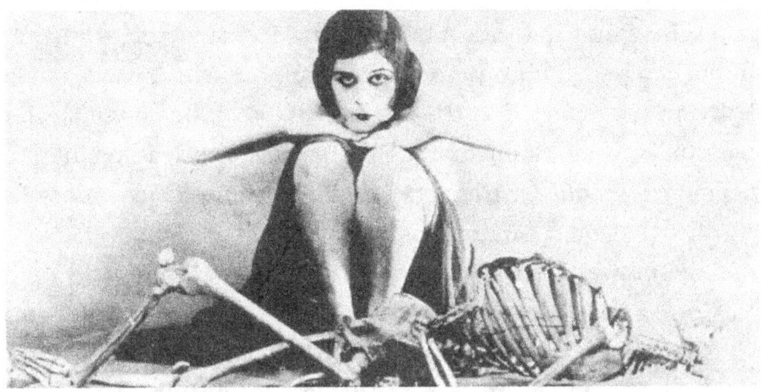

Theda Bara and the skeleton of one of her victims from the 1915 film *A Fool There Was.*

Film was still relatively new, and though it was quickly becoming clear that its ability to tell stories was more powerful than its predecessor, theater, various tricks of the industry today were in their infancy or simply did not exist. One of those was the power of publicity, whereby anyone could appear as was desired, provided the public believed it, or at least if they were uncertain of its veracity.

In a time when the spreading and finding of information was much slower and more difficult, William Fox (Wilhelm Fried Fuchs, Fried Vilmos, 1879 – 1952) and company presented Theodosia Goodman as a sinister figure, giving her a fictional past and personality in order to sell her mystique on the screen. Publicly it was claimed that her name "Theda" was an anagram of "death," and that her last name "Bara" a palindrome for "Arab," thus "Arab Death," an idea inspired by the popularity of the play *The Arab* (1911) by Edgar Selwyn (1875 –1944), which itself was its own cultural phenomenon. Bara's press agent would frequently provide journalists with various false stories about her, such as one that she was born "under the shadow of the Sphinx" (as reported in the June 1911 issue of *Photoplay Magazine*), and that her mother was a French actor, while her father was an Italian painter and sculptor who raised her in Babylon (as reported in the July 1917 issue of *Motography*). Her parents, it was claimed, taught her the arts leading her to become a famous Parisian stage actor, even in the legendary Le Théâtre du Grand Guignol (as reported in the August 1915 issue of *The Theatre*), which was known throughout the world from 1897 until its closure in 1962 as a theater of the macabre and sinister. When she was first revealed to the press in a private interview arranged by Fox, the lavish set on which she was introduced was certainly clear for the falsity it was to the reporters present but they, and eventually the public, would relish the fact that the woman possessed a powerful mystique, contrived though much of it actually was.

As early as 1915, such as in *Theatre Magazine* (Volume XXII) where she appears posing under a bat and in another photograph caressing a raven, her actual identity was well-documented, but stories of her past were increasingly exaggerated, including the claim that she was Cleopatra reincarnated when she starred in her most critically-acclaimed and successful film of the era, *Cleopatra* (1917), but the public was not entirely foolish in this regard, either. Much like the press at the time, they simply enjoyed the assumed mystery of Theda Bara, and the real details, at least at the time, were murky and difficult to determine for many, which only increased interest in her work and what she represented. With a slew of publicity photographs featuring her with serpents and skulls, Bara was solidified into public perception as the embodiment of a type of excessive, feminine vileness they simply adored. The vamp now had a face that almost everyone recognized.

Another original poster for *A Fool There Was* (1922).

A Fool There Was features a story similar to the previous novel and stage versions based on the painting "The Vampire" and Kipling's inspired poem, and was an immediate success in spite of facing competition from films such as David Wark Griffith's (known popularly as D. W. Griffith, 1875 – 1948) *The Birth of a Nation* or Cecil Blount DeMille's (known popularly as Cecil B. DeMille, 1881 –1959) *The Arab*. Bara not only became a star quicker than those before her, but her presentation of the Vampire started a cultural revolution. For its original premiere *A Fool There Was* was introduced by an actor who was hired to read Kipling's vampire poem before the viewing, apparently to increase the tension in the audience. Sections of Kipling's poem appear throughout the film as the plot develops, with Bara's absolutely sinister character connected with natural forces of nature, such as a storm. The film was also noted for its unhappy ending, a tradition that eschewed the norm of the time, which still stands in American filmmaking today and which the Russian film industry referred to as the "happy end" (simply meaning that everything tends to go well for good characters and bad for the evil ones). For Bara's film, the ending was not the usual standard audiences were used to, and her devious smiles and symbolic usages of flowers, including one scene where a former, ruined lover threatens to shoot her through the heart as she playfully taps the muzzle down with what appears to be a white rose, solidified her image. Perhaps the most famous moment of the entire film is the line "Kiss me, my fool," which appears shortly before the same man threatens to take his own life by placing a gun to his head, a choice he finalizes a few moments later. The ending, famously, features one of the lines from the Kipling poem reading "So some of him lived, but the most of him died," before a shot is shown of Bara raining flower petals on the presumably dead body of John Schulyer, ruined and collapsed on the floor. This is not long after his wife and child attempted to win him back with their love, but he is too easily lured into the grip of the Vampire, who in a newspaper article in the film is described as one of the "vampire species," connecting her with a cultural idea of the femme fatale, now under its new name. Other actresses, such as Olga Petrova (Muriel Harding, 1884 – 1977) would star in similar roles, such as her portrayal of a similar character in *The Vampire* (1915), but the majority of these examples are lost and though the actresses in them portrayed vamp characters, without access to at least fragments, the author has not considered them for analysis. As the next image shows, however, there are a variety of publicity photographs, posters, and stills that the reader may find if they take the time to discover more examples.

Advertisement for the American film *The Vampire* (1915).

Bara's career after *A Fool There Was* was as stormy as it was short. By 1918 she was arguably one of the five most important actors actresses in the United States and equally in the world. One can find articles of her in various publications in the early 1920s, such a brief discussion of the film from Volume 80 of *Life* in 1922, where Bara's portrayal of the vamp was considered culturally significant beyond the impact of any previous productions. Making slightly over forty films from 1914 until 1926, her popularity quickly waned, however, after the end of World War I (called the "Great War" by many at the time), due to changing public tastes concerning the vamp image and the cultural backlash against what Theda Bara embodied. The effects of the war were more far-reaching than some today may understand. Simply put, the horrors of modern war that destroyed the naivety of previous generations caused a cultural reaction that led to disinterest in images of wantonness, feminine or otherwise. Still, the idea of the vamp was already in place in spite of changing opinions on its prevalence. By 1919, though Bara's career was largely over, the public was greeted by a popular song adaptation of the vampire, Byron Sturges Gay's (1886 – 1945) "The Vamp" (1919), billed on the original sheet music as a "Novelty Oriental Fox Trot." The "Oriental" aspect was meant to capitalize on interest in Asia (and practically anything to the East of Western Europe) that was part of popular culture in England, Europe, and the United States since the Victorian era, lending to it an exotic quality. The lyrics of Gay's song read as follows, presenting the idea of the vamp as a dance.

Ev'rybody do the vamp,
Vamp until you get a cramp;
Grab your tootsie, hold her tight,
While they're playing, just keep swaying,

Do a little "what not", do a little fox trot,
When you cuddle up don't fight.
Vamp and swing along, keep a doing it,
Vamp and sing a song, don't you ruin it,
Do a nifty step, with lots of "pep"
And watch your reputation.
Do a "Bumble Bee", buzz around a bit,
Shake a wicked knee, she will fall for it,
Vamp all night and day,
Keep vamping till you vamp your cares away.

Ah! Ah! Ah! Ah! Ah! Ah!
Vamp the little lady, vamp the little lady,
Vamp the little lady, vamp the little lady,
Ah! Ah! Ah! Ah! Ah! Ah!
She will like it, maybe, she will like it, maybe,
She will like it, maybe, oh you pretty baby,
Ah! Ah! Ah! Ah! Ah! Ah!
Make it good and snappy, make it good and snappy,
make it good and snappy, make it good and snappy,
Ah! Ah! Ah! Ah! Ah! Ah! Ah! Ah!

Guess I got to go now, guess I got to go now,
'sev'rybody happy, 'sev'rybody happy, 'sev'rybody
    happy, sure. Good!

Soon thereafter the song appeared in recorded form via Joseph C. Smith (1883 – 1965) and his orchestra in 1919 from Victor on shellac (an early type of 78rpm record popular during the early 20th century). Following the lyrics of the original Byron Gay version, though in a slightly different order, the vocalist's mystical crooning of the line with "ah!" created an oppressive atmosphere balanced by the joyful patterns of the dance that could be sung with the tune. This particular song led to others, including *Laughing Vamp* (1920) which appeared on shellac in the same year featuring vaudeville performer Isabella Patricola (1886 – 1965) whose bizarre laughing in the chorus and her playful singing at the start present an interesting atmosphere while she calls "You have heard about the dreadful vampires today, they will vamp you, vamp you till they steal your heart away..."

This song, as well as others like "Sally Green The Village Vamp" (1920), which states the primary character was "vamping the constable," made it clear that the term "vamp" was household terminology, even a verb. In another example from an issue of *The Billboard* in December of 1920, cheap carnival dolls called "Little Mary" were advertised, the first style of which featured "Vamp Eyes." It is not clear what this means, but the suggestion seems to be that applying makeup to eyelashes was enough to become wanton. Or perhaps it was their shape and color, if we consider an issue of *The Optical Journal* from May 31st, 1923 where an optometrist supposedly stated that a vamp's eyes have a "large predominating setting" and that "most of them are dark."

In later songs like "Flamin' Mamie" (1925) or "Fascinatin' Vamp" (1928, an example of the original sheet music is shown in the next image) would utilize the vamp theme, absorbing it into the "Flapper" of the time, but retaining the original meaning made popular by Bara's various characters on screen of a young girl who could lead unsuspecting men, especially those chasing their lost youth, to ruin. The former song, for example, refers to the title character as a "heart scorcher" who "loves torture." Truly Bara's image in *A Fool there Was*, though gone by the early 1920s in film in preference for others, remained as a cultural presence that would outlive her own career. The image of the vamp remained in popular culture well into the late 1920s after Bara disappeared from acting and the power of its influence inspired many actresses into the 1950s, though they were not necessarily aware of the origins of their particular style of acting or the mannerisms they presented on screen.

As Bara's methods and character portrayals became standardized, they moved through Hollywood, the world, and among audiences like folklore. Movements of the eyes, smiles, and so forth became stock to the image of a devious, manipulative woman.

Cover of Charles H. Templeton, Sr. sheet music *Fascinatin' Vamp*, 1928.

So what, then, was the classic vamp? The vamp is most typically a young woman, who at first had long, dark hair, and whose sexual power was further honed by her intelligence and cunning in order to prey upon men she determined possessed something that she wanted. It was often for financial gain, using sexuality to keep her prey attached, regardless of whether or not it satisfied her on a physical level. The vast majority of vamp characters, thusly, were single women within urban settings, sometimes like the "cougar" image made popular in the early 2000s. There are also numerous examples of characters in other genres, such as westerns, that feature characteristics of the vamp quality and were referred to as such. Though not common, only occasional references to men as "vamps" can be located, most notably the ragtime song "Jelly Bean" (1920) which contains the following two opening lines: "Now there's a lady killing champ, He's just a soda water vamp..." This is rare, however, and most vamps were younger women. This image can be seen developing from a human being into a supernatural entity over time, retaining the vamp's primary feature of sexual power into the modern era, transforming it into something timeless and immortal, but with the same sinister control over her victims. The idea of the "human vampire" was soon to evolve. Note the advertisement for the film *Trifling Women* (1922), shown in the next image, for example.

Advertisement for the silent film *Trifling Women*, October 1, 1922.

After Bara and other actresses of the vamp tradition faded into film history, the image's cultural dominance remained, slowly absorbed by the supernatural entity called the vampire as it itself became a popular culture phenomenon. This did not truly become a reality until the 1930s. The simple explanation for this is that the supernatural image of popular culture was predominately male, much like the original folklore of pre-Christian Slavic belief, due to the transition from literature into theater, followed by film. The vast majority of literary vampires of the 19th century were male, such as Lord Ruthven (pronounced 'Riven') from Dr. John William Polidori's (1795 – 1821) *The Vampyre* (serialized and in book form in 1819) or the Penny Dreadful sensation "Varney the Vampire" from the mid-1840s, but there were three female vampires in the original Gothic period, the little-known "Brunhilda" from Ernst Raupach's (1784 – 1852) short story "Wake Not the Dead: A Fairytale" (1823), the recently discovered character "Heira" from the short story "The Vampire of Vourla" (1845, which includes the first known human-to-bat transformation in popular culture), or the more influential "Carmilla" from the novella by the same named (serialized and published in book form in 1871 and 1872) by Joseph Sheridan Le Fanu (1814 – 1873). Aside from these two primary examples, most vampires were older, aristocratic or high society men preying on young women. This cultural phenomenon extended to film primarily through the portrayal of Count Dracula by one individual, Béla Ferenc Dezső Blaskó (1882 – 1956), known by his chosen American name of "Bela Lugosi," who starred successfully as Dracula in the play of the same name by John Balderston (1889 – 1954) in 1927, edited from the original version by Hamilton Deane (1880 – 1958) that was popular in England starting in 1924. Lugosi's accent and exotic appearance soon solidified the now classic look of the character Dracula, but as in other horror films that would appear after the 1931 film adaptation of the novel and play, female vampires were merely under control of the male vampire that took precedence in the plot. Dracula was, in fact, the only established popular culture image of a supernatural vampire at that time.

Female vampires were primarily accessories and based loosely on the "weird sisters" of Stoker's original novel, themselves minor characters used only for brief shock value in two primary scenes in *Dracula* (1931). The only vampires on screen before Lugosi were extensions of the vamp phenomenon that came prior and which exploded with Theda Bara. Images based on this tradition would sometimes transfer supernatural-like qualities to the character, but only as part of the image.

The cover of *Life Magazine* from 1925 (shown on the next page), created by Coles Philips (1880–1927), is known as the "vampire girl" and "vampire flapper." Here the idea of the vampire is merely mingled with that of the flapper, and is not intended to represent a supernatural creature, but her bat-like costume imparts more of a mystical presence that suggests this.

"The Vampire Girl." Life Magazine, 1925. Coles Philips.

At the same time the flapper image was assuming traits from the vamp as well. An issue of *Variety* from July of 1926, for example, refers to new "collegiate slanguage" and briefly discusses the term "flamper," which is explained as a combination of flapper and vamp. Obviously, this idea of vamp qua flapper was not unique to Phillips' magazine cover and the public was readily making connections to the vamp image of the prior decade to the flapper of the then current one. Even later in the decade, in 1929, the term vamp was still popular, with the character "Babs" (a flapper-styled girl) from *So This is College*, referred to as a vamp by a critic in the December 24th issue of the "Circleville Herald." Thus, even after a decade, the image was still recognized and established in publications and colloquial speech.

This would begin to change in a minor horror film starring Lugosi from 1935, *Mark of the Vampire*. Originally titled *Vampires of Prague*, the plot includes a vampire named Count Mora (played by Lugosi who speaks no lines until the end) and his "daughter" Luna, played by Carroll Borland (1914 – 1994, most typically known under her stage name of 'Carol Borland'), who was linked with Lugosi upon becoming acquainted with him after seeing him perform on stage as Dracula in 1929. According to an issue of the *Berkeley Daily Gazette* from December of 1932, her acting background was rather minimal at the time, restricted to work in high school and at the University of California, Berkeley, where, as a freshman, she was part of the school's theater company. This background, and her connections to Lugosi, led to her portrayal of "Lucy Westerna" in a tabloid (or "tab") production of *Dracula* in 1932 where he, according to the same source, was the director. Marian Marsh (Violet Ethelred Krauth, 1913 – 2006, who at the time often went by the name of 'Marion'), as established actress from roles in films such as *Svengali* (1931), supposedly was also considered for the role, but was passed over for Carroll Borland. Regardless of prior connections, as Luna in *Mark of the Vampire* she defined what the female vampire would become in supernatural form with her shroud-like dress and long, black hair parted in the middle. In many ways she was like the vamp image of the 1910s. The look of Luna became the typical female vampire image after 1935, inspiring later depictions as far as "Morticia" in *The Addams Family* (the TV series from 1964 to 1966, as well as the original comics and modern adaptations). Regardless, Luna was the first "technical" female vampire in media, meaning a supernatural entity and one that was not human, though the twist ending of *Mark of the Vampire* reveals otherwise when Lugosi and Borland inform the audience, indirectly, that they were merely actors playing actors playing vampires to fool a killer. For the majority of the film, however, Luna is presented as something other than human, and the allure of this character type would further grow in the 1930s, bringing along with it the traits of the classic vamp as the flapper image itself died and the supernatural took further root as the United States recovered from the Great Depression.

Luna's primary presence in *Mark of the Vampire* is one of the shadows. She only appears for fleeting moments, typically looming in the night with a sinister stare upon her face, speaking, as does Lugosi, only a few lines in the entire film, specifically at the end when the twist is revealed. When appearing she is presented as having dominance over her victims, but this is, as later revealed, all part of the act. Still, it is important to note that this female vampire, though not technically supernatural, is largely in control of her own actions in the film, as the viewer believes she is preying on a young woman in particular in a fashion similar to Sheridan Le Fanu's Carmilla. Though not what any scholar would consider a "lesbian vampire", Luna exudes a sense of dominance and control much unlike the vampire "wives" of Dracula in *Dracula* (1931) where Lugosi has, instead, seemingly full command of their actions. It was this sense of vamp-era dominance in Luna that would define the female vampire thereafter. Most significantly after *Mark of the Vampire* for the vamp-into-vampire image came Universal Studios' sequel to *Dracula, Dracula's Daughter* (1936), most recently the inspiration of the film *Abigail* (2024, the reader should note it is not a remake).

Sources from 1936 and 1937 indicate the film was "based on the original story by Bram Stoker" (see, for example, the *Scientific Canadian Mechanics' Magazine and Patent Office Record*, Volume 64, Part 1, 1936), which specifically refers to the short story first published after Stoker's death under the name "Dracula's Guest" in the collection *Dracula's Guest and Other Weird Stories* (1914). The story is what little remains of the original first three chapters of *Dracula*, which were removed to condense the plot and cheapen the cost of production and the cover price.

The film version derived from Stoker's story, *Dracula's Daughter*, is based but loosely on the work, focusing on a female vampire as the primary protagonist, as well as antagonist. The titular character in the 1936 film, "Countess Zaleska," played by Gloria Holden (1903 – 1991), is presented as a conflicted, gender-marginal, sympathetic character interested, at least at first, in removing her own curse to be, "free to live as a woman" (roughly at timestamp 13:48 depending on the version viewed). Though her attempts at the start of the film are notable for the sympathy they evoke in the viewer, she, in the end, succumbs to her curse and in order to control a man and transform him into her vampire slave, uses a young girl as a tool in the process. In consideration of earlier parts of this essay, one should note Holden's portrayal of Zaleska, after her sympathetic phase, echoes the dominating, cold figure of the vamp of the silent era. Holden was largely presenting the character in the style of actresses in over two decades of film, whether or not she was aware. Sources available from the first appearance of the film in 1936 to later showings in the early 1940s give no indication of the fact and only focus on the film's presentation.

Poster for *Dracula's Daughter* (1936).

The difference in comparison to what came before, thematically, was that *Dracula's Daughter* was the first time a truly supernatural vamp-like vampire woman was presented on screen, with elements reminiscent of the character Carmilla and sexually liminal overtones. The so-called "first" adaptation of *Carmilla* in the German film *Vampyr* (1932), is overstated, and inaccurate. It was, in fact, an adaptation of Sherdian Le Fanu's work *In a Glass Darkly* (first published in 1872), with a quasi-vampire never called Carmilla, and much older. Gloria Holden as Countess Zaleska, however, was much like the fully-human vamp of the silent era and through the 1920s, but now the sexual allure and powers of this being were attached to the vampire itself, and this tradition would continue, largely speaking, into the modern era. Zaleska, though referred to by some modern scholars as the first "lesbian vampire" on screen, is ultimately using women to enslave a man, making her more bisexual than anything, though Universal Studios was sure to exploit her unclear sexual identity in advertising, with some posters stating: "She gives you that WEIRD FEELING!"

After *Dracula's Daughter*, much like images of the male vampire in media as it stepped from literature, the female vampire, with its attachments to early presentations of the vamp in the silent era, started to adapt to changing cultural climates. In *Son of Dracula* (1943), for example, the character "Katherine" presents the typical vamp allure with her piercing eyes and dominating voice. In fact, in the original trailer for the film, she is introduced as "the screen's most fascinating woman vampire, luring men with cold beauty." This simple phrasing, in itself, is exactly the idea of the original vamp of the 1910s and representative of its cultural impact. Female vampires largely reflect this tradition, even today, outside of occasional references to the classic camp, such as the 1955 Broadway musical comedy, *The Vamp*, which referenced many ideas from the

1910s. Most vampire characters from 1936 until the late 1960s were of darker hair, but into the 1970s as discussions of *Carmilla* and Countess Elizabeth Báthory de Ecsed (Báthori Erzsébet, 1560/1561 – 1614), from which she was partially inspired, became commonplace, female vampires started to combine features of both and the general concept of a dominating woman was the typical theme, regardless of physical appearance, or even age. Polish-born actress Ingrid Pitt (Ingoushka Petrov, 1937 – 2010), most importantly portrayed both Carmilla in *The Vampire Lovers* (1970) and then Elizabeth Bathory in *Countess Dracula* (1971), setting off a new revolution of the vamp image through supernatural characters that drew from the cultural effects of Second-Wave Feminism, then known as "Women's Liberation," "Women's Lib," or simply "Lib" for short. The number of Carmilla and Bathory films in the 1970s is almost startling, including the notorious *Vampyros Lesbos* (1971), but can be easily read as simple extensions of Theda Bara's vamp into supernatural territory over time with more explicit exploitation of the female body in a decade of opening sexuality.

Films such as *The Devil's Wedding Night* (*Il plenilunio delle vergini*, 1973) portray a character that combines Carmilla and Bathory into essentially one image named "La Contessa Dolingen de Vries," whereas others such as *The Blood Spattered Bride* (*La novia ensangrentada*, 1979) focused on the Carmilla image entirely. Regardless of the title or theme, all of these films continue the sexually charged, and manipulative, woman of danger from the earlier part of the 20th century. As time moved further, it was this image in particular that was most dominant so that, even today, the female vampire tends to have a larger focus on her sexual power as a weapon, and her seductiveness echoes Bara's silent allure in practically any form of media imaginable. From Vampirella in the realm of comic books (1969 to present) to Alcina Dimitrescu and her daughters in *Resident Evil Village* (2021), this image of the cold and calculative woman became more permanent than anyone would have likely realized over a century ago, and it will likely continue into the unforeseeable future. What started as a set of curious circumstances, eventually, became a powerful phenomenon.

Notable Vamps and the Vamp's Cultural Impact in Film

The reader should note the difficulty in constructing this final section, which is not intended, by any means, to be exhaustive. Its purpose is to provide an idea of different portrayals of vamps or vamp-like characters in the critical period from 1915 until 1929 when the vamp was most dominant, utilizing the most important stars of the era and others who are lesser-known. Some of the actresses presented here, with short biographies and selected films for viewing, were not necessarily referred to as vamps specifically, but they presented a character in at least one film that is arguably connected to this tradition. At times the presentation is more of a seductive, or playful allure than the calculating predator exemplified in the 1910s, but these connections are visible nonetheless as the flapper image assumed traits from its predecessor. The actresses are presented in alphabetical order with basic biographical information and representative films that include a vamp character or character presentations thematically connected to the idea. Only films with at least surviving fragments that are currently accessible, including trailers that display vamps or similar characters, were included, and are presented in order of release date. The availability of various films led to the particular selection of actresses presented here, as well as a close look at portrayals referred to as vamps to some capacity.

Illustrated cover from *The Siren's Song* (1919) sheet music, with image of Theda Bara.

Owing to this approach, a number of famous vamp productions such as *A Virtuous Vamp* (1919 comedy) starring Constance Talmadge (1898 – 1973), as well as lesser-known examples like *The Law and the Woman* (1922) starring Betty Compson (1897 – 1974), are not presented here due to a lack of viewing materials or lack of adherence to the theme, such as the character "Belle the Blonde" from *The Half-Breed* (1916), played by Winifred Westover (1899 – 1978), who called the character "Baby Blue Eyes" and declared her in a 1929 interview a "dance hall vamp," though the character bears little connection to the image. This focus on a film's availability assisted in reducing the list substantially. Further, films past 1929 have not been included as this is passing the era when the vamp image was most visible, in spite of its perseverance through altered forms thereafter. 1929 as the end date is two-fold because it is soon to be the current year of public domain for any creations released in 1929 and prior. This means that all films here are legally public domain by 2025, but most are already within this legal standard in 2024. All the images used in this section are copyright free as well and the films suggested for viewing are readily available for free, in many cases in totality, in digital format. The reader is encouraged to research other actresses of the era who were known for playing vamp characters to learn more about the presence of the image, for there are many examples in publicity photos and old magazine articles about films, but for this publication the author had, by necessity, to be selective. The goal here was to be representative, and not concise. Other than public domain information about the actresses in this section, the vast majority of information was gleaned by the author's immersion in the time utilizing old movie magazines from the 1910s and 1920s, as well as some from later dates, for references and to fact-check various statements, blurbs, and so forth that can be found online, making these biographies, though short, the most accurate the reader is likely to find in this format. Any sources used are clearly indicated.

Josephine Baker
Freda Josephine Baker, née McDonald, 1906 — April 12, 1975

Josephine Baker in *La Sirène des Tropiques* by G. Rader, c. 1927, chromolithograph on paper, from the National Portrait Gallery.

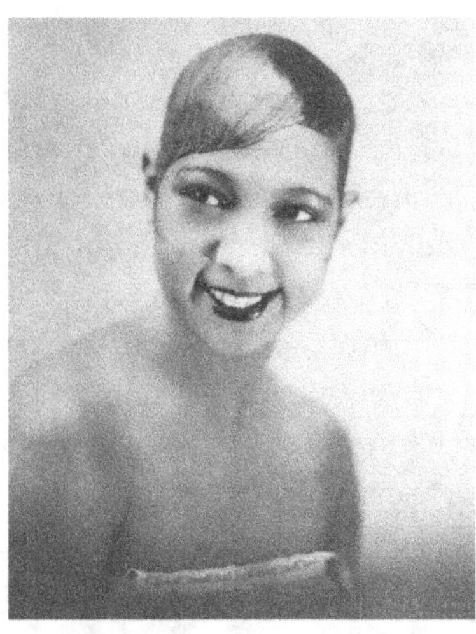

Josephine Baker, portrait by Henri Manuel circa 1920.

Josephine Baker's early life is somewhat clouded, and the majority of early publications into the 1940s detail very little about her life. As an actress, like many African Americans, her potential reach in the United States at the time was extremely limited. Early black cinema was largely unknown outside of African American communities, and even stars who were able to secure roles in bigger productions were typically relegated to stereotypical depictions of characters like the "mammy" type, among others. Baker, further, like some of the actresses discussed here, did not start in acting but in dance. The majority we know of her came originally from the biography *Josephine: The Hungry Heart* (1993), written by her foster son Jean-Claude Baker (Jean-Claude Julien Léon Tronville, 1943 – 2015), who stated her father was likely white, but the fact was never officially revealed and the truth likely died with Baker's mother, Carrie, who herself was adopted by a former slave with potential Native American roots named Elvira. Jean-Claude said himself that, at times, elements of his mother's remembrances were incorrect. Thus, some of her past is unknown, though it is well-established that she grew up in a poor community in St. Louis, Missouri, eventually working for various wealthy white families in the area and experiencing all the ugliness of the era's racism, including the "East St. Louis Massacre" of 1917. At times, Baker even lived on the streets, earning small amounts of money by performing on corners, but these early steps into entertainment provided fertile ground for her future. Her earliest professional work was for various vaudeville productions in St. Louis starting at the age of thirteen, eventually leading her to New York during the "Harlem Renaissance" by 1925, though she was not officially connected to this cultural revolution until much later in her career.

Her break in acting was due to her connection with a few African American entertainers, such as Florence Mills (Florence Winfrey, 1896 – 1927), who was a success at the "Plantation Club" in Manhattan. This was Baker's first experience with professional dancing, as she was given the opportunity to perform at the same club and eventually in *Shuffle Along* (1921, first presentation) as one of the chorus girls in a production in New Haven, Connecticut, before performing in New York City by the time she was seventeen. According to her foster son, Baker would, at times, begin to perform in her own way to draw more attention to herself, including crossing her eyes, and this led to further recognition of her personality and skill. It was not on Broadway, however, that she would achieve her fame, where she found herself constantly placed into the line of chorus girls in spite of her unique presentations. Baker eventually left for Paris, France in 1925, where she would become recognized worldwide through connections to other African American emigrees such as "Bricktop" (nickname of Ada Beatrice Queen Victoria Louise Virginia Smith, 1894 – 1984). Along with her dancing, which included erotic elements in her European performances, Baker also engaged in singing, but for film she found success only in Europe, starting in the 1920s. Her first appearances were actually filmed versions of dance routines, but for acting her first role was "Papitou" in *Siren of the Tropics* (*La Sirène des tropiques*, 1927). Somewhat close to the vamp image, the film is notable for extending Baker's career further, as it was connected with her dancing at the time, and for its connections to the flapper image of the 1920s. Following this, she starred in the German-French co-production of *The Woman from Folies Bergères* (*Die Frauen von Folies Bergères*, 1927), but it should be understood these earlier performances were something of extensions of her dancing persona.

By the 1930s she starred in more significant roles, such as *Zou-Zou* (1934), where she starred as the title character in the first role in history to feature a black woman as the prominent star. This is, however, outside of the scope of our timeline. Much of Baker's career was connecting to her dancing, and her vamp-like persona was largely the public's interpretation of her stage presence, which sometimes featured erotic elements. Through the rest of her life her affairs are well-documented, which the reader is encouraged to locate, but her career in the 1920s was only the beginning of her popularity. She would eventually die of a cerebral hemorrhage in 1975. The reader should note that the films selected here are somewhat tenuous in their connection to the vamp image, but Baker's erotic persona was most certainly recognized, albeit subconsciously, as linked to the idea, though no early publications ever refer to her as a "vamp" properly speaking. In addition, her popularity undoubtedly affected the careers of other actresses of the time, including Nina Mae McKinney (1912 – 1967), the so-called "Black Garbo" (see Greta Garbo for the significance of this phrasing) whose work primarily flourished in the 1930s.

Stanley Stepanic

Filmography

- *Folies Bergères* (various dancing shorts, some of uncertain dates)
- *Siren of the Tropics* (*La Sirène des tropiques*, 1927)
- *The Fireman of the Folies Bergères* (*Le pompier des Folies Bergères*, erotic short, 1928)

Theda Bara
Theodosia Burr Goodman, 1885 – 1955

A poster from *The She-Devil* (1918), starring Theda Bara.

Theda Bara , portrait by Orval Hixon, 1921.

Theda Bara portrayed the original, most culturally significant vamp in history, though she was by no means the first. Due to a thorough discussion of her in the essay presented in this book, we will be briefer for this biography in comparison to the rest. Born on July 29th to Bernard Goodman (1853 – 1936), a Jewish tailor from Poland, and Pauline Louise Françoise de Coppet (1861 – 1957), a French Swiss, Bara started acting at age eighteen, roughly twelve years before she achieved fame in *A Fool There Was*. Many of her films are lost, while others exist only in fragments. Only six of her forty-three known films have survived. Two, *Cleopatra* and *Salome*, exist only in fragments, but *A Fool There Was*, which exemplifies the vamp, thankfully survives in totality. All three of these examples present the vamp in classic form.

Filmography

- *A Fool There Was* (1915)
- *Cleopatra* (1917)
- *Salome* (1918)

Elisabeth Bergner
1897 – 1986

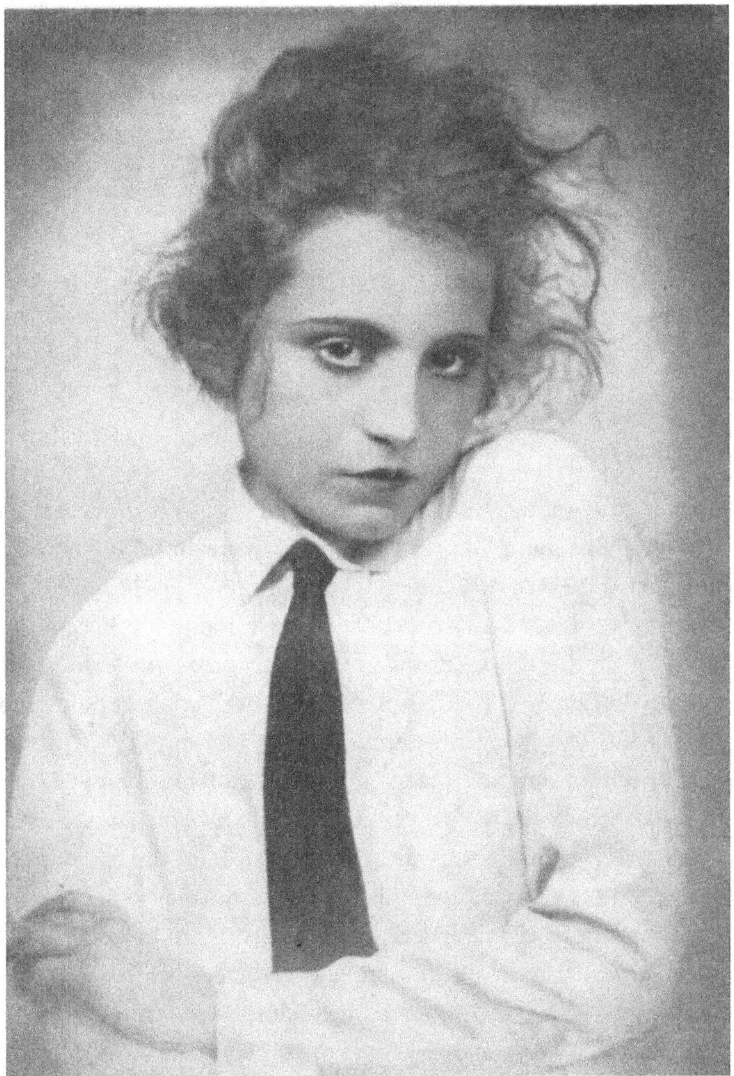

Elisabeth Bergner in *Fräulein Julie* (1922).

Elisabeth Bergner, circa 1924. Billy Rose
Theatre Division, The New York Public
Library.

Born in the Austro-Hungarian Empire in what is today part of
Ukraine, Elisabeth Bergner's parents were both Jewish; her
mother Anna Rosa Wagner married Emil Schmelke Juda and
the pair eventually changed their last name to Bergner to
sound more German. Known in Germany prior to World War II
as "Die Bergner" ("The Bergner"), Elisabeth spent a portion of
her earlier life living in Vienna. In 1911 she entered a private
acting school and soon thereafter the Academy for the Music
and Performing Arts (Universität für Musik und Darstellende
Kunst Wien). Her debut was on stage in 1915 at the age of fourteen. By 1916 she was living in Zürich and became acquainted
with members of the artistic community there before moving
back to Vienna in 1918. Actively involved in the Austrian
Communist Party, Bergner continued to act, known for her
"trouser role" characters (characters played by the opposite
sex), until a guest appearance with Hans Walter Conrad Veidt
(Conrad Veidt, 1893 – 1943) led her towards film in Berlin. Her
first role was as "Magdalena" in *The Evangelist* (*Der*

Evangelimann, 1924) and her continual stage presence in Berlin led her to become the highest paid actress in the city at the time. This period, sometimes referred to by scholars as the "Bergner Phenomenon," reveals the cultural impact of the actress in the era. She was known for presenting characters that were fragile yet intelligent and wily, creating an erotic, androgynous form of screen starlet. After marrying Hungarian-born British director Paul Czinner (1890 – 1972), she starred in his film *The Rise of Catherine the Great* (1934). But owing to her Jewish heritage, Bergner found her status, and films, under violent scrutiny as the Nazi Party rose in power. After assisting other Jewish actors to flee Germany, *The Rise of Catherine the Great* was met by a political riot started by the Nazis when it debuted in Berlin, and the event received attention of the British Parliament, which led her to England. Later, Bergner attempted to return to acting in the United States after fleeing England due to fears of Nazi invasion, a move for which she was criticized. Finding limited success in the states other than a critically acclaimed run on Broadway, she moved back to London by 1950 due to rising Cold War tensions and her connections to the Communist Party. Starring off and on the stage until her death in 1985 from cancer, Bergner's last film was the West German production *Fine Company – Limited Liability* (*Feine Gesellschaft - Beschränkte Haftung*, 1982). She only starred in six films before the 1930s. Most have elements of the vamp, but only three are easily accessible.

Filmography

- *Husbands or Lovers* (*Nju - Eine unverstandene Frau*, 1924)
- *The Violinist of Florence* (*Der Geiger von Florenz*, 1926)
- *Miss Else* (*Fräulein Else*, 1929)

Olive Borden
Olive Mary Borden, 1906 – 1947

Olive Borden portrait from *Photo-Play Magazine*, October 1926.

Olive Borden in *Cine Mundial Magazine*, March 1929.

Born in Richmond, Virginia, and a distant cousin of Lizzie Andrew Borden (1860 – 1927), Olive Borden's life is one of the more tragic stories of early Hollywood. Known for her exquisite beauty and raven-black hair, she rose to fame in the 1920s and quickly fell, forgotten by many of her associates and once close friends. Aside from a long-standing mystery concerning her "real name," which was mistakenly believed to be "Sybil Tinkle" until the early 1990s, her life is less mystery, more tragedy. Her father died when she was an infant and her mother Cecelia raised her in Norfolk, Virginia, then later Baltimore, Maryland. At the age of fifteen Borden received her first film credits in comedy shorts by Mack Sennett (Michael Sinnott, 1880 – 1960) known as the "Sennett Bathing Beauties," as well as comedy shorts by Harold Eugene "Hal" Roach Sr. (known popularly as "Hal Roach," 1892 – 1992). Sennett, who worked with some the most famous comedians of the silent era, would incorporate random, bikini-clad young women for these shorts, but Borden would not properly appear as a vamp character until her work with Hal Roach. Borden's career was promising by 1925 when she signed a contract with Fox, becoming one of their highest paid actresses until her contract was reduced in 1927. This was after she starred in the famous film *The Joy Girl* (1927), which earned her the nickname "The Joy Girl." Unfortunately, thereafter Borden faced issues securing comparable contracts, had difficulty transitioning to sound as many of her era, and her private life was soiled by numerous scandals. For example, her first husband, Theodore Isadore Spector (1899 – 1966), was arrested for bigamy in 1934 when it was revealed he never divorced his first wife. Such affairs, and an issue with spending too freely, led to a progressive downfall for Borden just as quickly as she rose. After refusing a pay cut with Fox in 1927, she was never able to reclaim her popularity in spite of several successful films up into the 1940s, growing more and more destitute. By the end she was living with her mother in the "Sunshine Mission," a charity house in skid row in Los Angeles. After running from the mission, she was found living alone in a dilapidated hotel and then returned yet would die penniless with liver problems in 1947. According to Michelle Vogel in *Olive Borden: The Life and Films of Hollywood's "Joy Girl,"* she stated in her final interview a day prior to her death: "The whole world has fallen in on me." A number of her films are lost, but, thankfully, some of the vamp type (or with closely connected imagery) have survived.

Filmography

- *Too Many Mammas* (1924)
- *Should Husbands Be Watched?* (1925)
- *3 Bad Men* (1926)
- *Fig Leaves* (1926)

- *The Monkey Talks* (1927)
- *Half Marriage* (1929)
- *Dance Hall* (1929)

Clara Bow
Clara Gordon Bow, 1905 – 1965

Image from a lobby card for the film *It* (1927) starring Clara Bow.

Clara Bow, 1928. Photograph by J. Willis Sayre.

After Theda Bara, Clara Bow is arguably the most important image of "sex appeal" from classic Hollywood. Born in the slums of Brooklyn in 1905, her mother and maternal grandmother were both mentally ill. Her father, disinterested in children or marriage, was generally absent from her life. There is some debate about her birth due to inconsistencies, such as her crypt marker reading "July 29, 1907," but 1905 is the accepted date. Her early life was filled with degradation and poverty, such as a rape by her father around the age of sixteen while her mother, Sarah, would supplement the family's meager income with prostitution when Bow's father would enter states of drunken disinterest. At the time roughly half of the population of the United States went to the movies, as the art had gone from its realist infancy into storytelling that was slowly overtaking theater. Bow, like many Americans, found escape in the medium, and soon dreamed of entering Hollywood. By chance, in 1921, she entered a "Fame and Fortune" contest using a cheap tintype (old photographs done on metal) that subsequently won her the prize, which was officially announced in January of 1922. Part of the prize was her casting in the 1922 film *Beyond the Rainbow*, which soon led to minor and then more significant roles that eventually expanded exponentially via the 1927 film *It*. The term "it" was a euphemism for "sex" at the time, and Clara Bow became the legendary "it girl" after the success of her namesake film, in spite of a range of roles prior and noted excellence in the acting profession. Regardless, Bow was often viewed as an outsider by Hollywood elite due to her upbringing and general behavior. In the October issue of *Photoplay* from 1929, for example, she famously stated: "I'm a curiosity in Hollywood. I'm a big freak because I'm myself!" Constantly irritated by the falsity of the Hollywood elite, she would regardless survive the transition into sound pictures in the late 1920s and early 1930s, though eventually financial mistakes, scandals, and mental illness led her into seclusion, dying of heart problems in 1965. Though Bow was never referred to widely as a "vamp," several of her roles were of flapper characters that exemplified the attitude and style that had been set by prior vamps of the silver screen. Further, due to the connection of the vamp to the flapper image of the 1920s, Bow's presentations of various characters continue a style similar to wanton women of Hollywood in the 1910s to which the flapper attached. Some of her films, such as *Wine* (1924, her first starring role), are considered lost, but many examples survive that the reader may consider for analysis.

Filmography

- *Black Oxen* (1923)
- *Daughters of Pleasure* (1924)
- *Empty Hearts* (1924)
- *My Lady's Lips* (1925)

- *Parisian Love* (1925)
- *The Keeper of the Bees* (1925)
- *The Primrose Path* (1925)
- *Free to Love* (1925)
- *My Lady of Whims* (1925)
- *The Plastic Age* (1925)
- *Mantrap* (1926)
- *It* (1927)
- *Children of Divorce* (1927)
- *Rough House Rosie* (1927)
- *Hula* (1927)
- *Get Your Man* (1927)
- *Red Hair* (1928)
- *The Wild Party* (aka *Stella's Merits*, 1929)

Lili Damita
Liliane Marie-Madeleine Carré, 1904 – 1994

Image from a movie star postcard featuring Lili Damita, published by Ross Verlag in 1928, photograph by Alexander Binder.

Image from *Cine-Mundial*, December 1928.

Born in France, Lili Damita worked briefly in dance and modeling. After taking part in a beauty contest in 1921 she received an offer for a film role in *Maman Pierre* (1922). This led to a variety of roles in Europe, almost twenty, before she emigrated to the United States to play a role in *The Escape* (1929). Her first lead role was in the Austrian silent film *Das Spielzeug von Paris* (known typically in English as *Red Heels*, 1925). Shortly thereafter sound films (nicknamed "talkies" initially in the United States) became the norm, but Damita found the transition rather easy into this new form of film in spite of her thick accent, and would star in almost twenty additional productions until she retired. Though skilled in her own right, Lili Damita is primarily remembered for the man she married in 1935, Errol Flynn (Errol Leslie Thomson Flynn, 1909 – 1959), a notorious womanizer and voyeur in spite of his fame in Hollywood's "Golden Age." Their tempestuous relationship was eventually more recognized than Damita's roles as her husband rose to infamy after a statutory rape case in 1942 a few months after their divorce. According to sources such as Ellis

Amburn's *Olivia de Havilland and the Golden Age of Hollywood* (2018) Damita and Flynn had an incredible sexual connection, but their relationship outside of these moments was extremely tempestuous. Their only son, Sean Flynn (1941 – 1984), a known Vietnam photojournalist, was Damita's primary concern in life until his disappearance in Cambodia in 1970. She declared him dead in 1984 and more recent attempts to recover his remains, including one in 2010, were fruitless. Many of her films survive, but only one of the vamp type exists that is accessible.

Filmography

- *Das Spielzeug von Paris* (*The Toy of Paris*, known also as *Red Heels*, 1925)

Lya de Putti
Amália Helena Mária Róza Putti,
Putti Amália Helena Mária Róza, 1897 — 1931

Image from a movie star postcard featuring Lya de Putti, published by Ross
Verlag in 1928, photograph by Alexander Binder.

Still from *The Sorrows of Satan* (1926).

Born in Vojčice, Slovakia, which was then a town that was part of the Austro-Hungarian Empire under the name of Vécse, Lya de Putti was part of a noble lineage. Her mother, Mária Rozália Kamilla (1868 – 1945) was a Countess, and recognized an unruly nature in her daughter from an early age. Education at a convent did not have the desired effect of transforming her, so thinking an early marriage would quell her passions, de Putti was married at the age of fifteen. In spite of a comfortable life and two children, she continued to seek her fame in acting, discovered by Béla Balogh (1885 – 1945), one of the most important directors in Hungary in the 1910s until 1919. Impressed by the dancer's beauty, he cast her in the lead role in *Soldiers of the Emperor* (*A császár katonái*, 1918), which led the press to refer to de Putti as the Hungarian version of Pola Negri (see separate entry). Unfortunately, the post-World War I cultural and political climate, which led to the short-lived Hungarian Socialist State, the "Hungarian Soviet Republic," or literally the "Socialist Federalist Republic of Councils in

Hungary" (Magyarországi Szocialista Szövetséges Tanácsköztársaság, March to August 1919), temporarily stagnated the Hungarian film market and de Putti was overshadowed by other stars while some of her films were banned due to the new political climate. She found more success in Germany due to the connections between both countries' film industries at the time and in Berlin she was recognized for her dancing, which led to appearances in various small roles in German film.

This path culminated in a more substantial role in *The Love Affairs of Hector Dalmore* (*Die Liebschaften des Hektor Dalmore*, 1921), where she starred alongside Hans Walter Conrad Veidt (Conrad Veidt, 1893 – 1943). At the time Pola Negri was one of the most important actresses in Germany, but upon taking a Hollywood contract in 1923 the vacuum left behind was filled quite easily by de Putti who by 1924 was starring in vamp roles. Of her various films, *Variety* (*Varieté*, 1925), gained the attention of Paramount Studios in New York, and she accepted a contract and moved to the United States. Unfortunately, de Putti's aristocratic background and presence led her to be typecast in vamp roles, such as *The Sorrows of Satan* (1926), where in the German cut she appeared topless. Eventually disgusted with these characterizations, she moved to Hollywood in 1927. In a brief discussion in *Theatre* from 1927, it was stated that de Putti came from Hungary to "teach the American ladies some new tricks in the art of 'vamping'," but that she also accepted the abandonment of her vamp persona "joyously." Her first film in Hollywood, *The Heart Thief* (1927), was unfortunately not well-received and a reportedly a commercial disaster, leading her to a series of failures including one comedy. Inundated with more vamp roles, de Putti eventually went through plastic surgery to change the shape of her nose, then accepted contracts in Germany, then Hollywood once more, before starring in the successful British film *The Informer* (1929). A partial talkie, the film revealed de Putti's weaknesses with the introduction of sound components, and her voice was dubbed over by another actress, which further discouraged her. It was to be her last film. As the original vamp image died by the end of the 1920s, de Putti found herself increasingly forgotten, which caused a further descent into depression, leading to two apparent suicide attempts, though this was never officially verified. In a supposed state of mental illness, she swallowed a chicken bone, the removal of which eventually caused her to die of pneumonia. Her earlier films contain slight vamp elements, the reader should note, but she does not fully realize this form until *Variety*. Earlier films are provided, however, due to their accessibility and connections to the theme.

Filmography

- *The Indian Tomb* (*Das indische Grabmal*, 1921)
- *Othello* (1922)
- *The Burning Soil* (*Der brennende Acker*, 1922)
- *Phantom* (1922)
- *Variety* (1925)
- *Manon Lescaut* (1926)
- *The Sorrows of Satan* (1926)

Kay Francis
Katharine Edwina Gibbs, 1905 – 1968

Image from *New Movie Magazine* featuring Kay Francis, published in December 1929, photograph by Otto Dyar.

Kay Francis' career started to develop at the tail-end of the vamp phenomenon. Her fame largely came from various films she starred in in the 1930s, which in at least some cases continued this tradition, though as stated earlier we will not be considering films after 1929. Raised by a single mother who left her flippant father in 1908, she was only moderately successful on stage before gaining minor roles at Paramount until she was contracted by Warner Bros. in 1932 for *Man Wanted* to become their highest-paid star by 1935. Unfortunately, due to depression stemming from a scandalous private life, and after a disappointing return on the film *The White Angel* (1936), she was relegated back to the same fashion-focused film characters she had performed as in years prior. Due to this, often accepting roles others would not, the issue of rhotacism, and difficulties securing other roles outside of Warner Bros., Francis filed a suit against the studio and was soon thereafter dubbed, famously, "box office poison," when the Independent Theater Owners Association placed a paid-for ad in *The Hollywood Reporter* in 1938 claiming that Francis, and others, were financial liabilities for the industry. For uncertain reasons she backed down in the suit, and agreed to finish out her career in B pictures. Though she eventually experienced a minor comeback in the late 1930s when she contracted with RKO Radio Pictures (known as RKO, 1929 – 1959), her descent was gradual and tied into her personal life. Her acting career ended on stage and before she died, as was later discovered in her personal diaries (available at Wesleyen University), she stated: "When I die, I want to be cremated so that no sign of my existence is left on this earth. I can't wait to be forgotten" (from an entry dated 1938). In all of her filmography there is only one film in which she portrays the vamp, starring alongside Clara Bow (see separate entry). This particular film, where she plays a character named "Zara Flynn," is provided below.

Filmography

- *Dangerous Curves* (1929)

Greta Garbo
Greta Lovisa Gustafsson, 1905 – 1990

Photograph of Greta Garbo by Henry B. Goodwin circa 1920.

Greta Garbo in 1925, by Alexander Binder.

The youngest of three children of Anna Lovisa (née Johansson, 1872 – 1944) and Karl Alfred Gustafsson (1871 – 1920), Greta Garbo was part of a poor working-class family living in a poverty-ridden portion of Stockholm, Sweden. Known for her melancholic persona, Garbo's childhood, in particular the gray and dismal surroundings in which she was raised, undoubtedly had an effect on her acting later in life. Though she was interested in theater from childhood, and would engage other children in acting games, it was not until she found her first employment in 1920 as a salesclerk at the department store named "Pub" in her hometown that Garbo first tasted the lure of the profession. After posing as a hat model, and then general fashion model, she starred in at least two known advertising shorts, and was soon thereafter discovered by director Erik A. Petschler (1881 – 1945), who selected her for a minor role in a comedy short entitled *Peter the Tramp* (*Luffar-Petter*, 1922, ten minutes of which survive). This led her to enter The Royal Dramatic Training Academy (Kungliga Dramatiska Teaterns

Elevskola, also known as Dramatens Elevskola), where all leading Swedish actors at the time trained. Following this she gained her first leading role in *The Saga of Gösta Berling* (*Gösta Berlings Saga*, 1924), which was a commercial and critical success. This film in particular led Garbo to receive the attention of Louis Burt Mayer (Lazar Meir, 1884 – 1957), then vice president of Metro-Goldwyn-Mayer. Upon arriving in Hollywood in 1925, Garbo spoke very little English and languished in the area until she was contracted by MGM. Her first American film was *Torrent* (1926), and after her next film, *The Temptress* (1926), she was a recognized star internationally.

By her final film of the 1920s, *The Kiss* (1929), all of Garbo's films were commercial successes. MGM was concerned about her transition to sound pictures, however, as the new form of film ruined the careers of many actors from Europe in the 1930s. Garbo, however, found even more notoriety following the introduction of sound, though by the 1940s her increasing eccentricities (noted in several issues of *Life* in the 1930s and 1940s) and waning youth made acquiring further roles difficult. Though she did not die as destitute, in fact she was the highest paid actress at MGM for a large portion of her career; Garbo became increasingly reclusive and uncertain of her purpose. For most of her life as an adult she was alone, never marrying, and never having children, but her naturalistic, brooding acting style made her a star and her name is still resonant in Hollywood even today. She eventually died of pneumonia and renal failure and her ashes were returned to her native Sweden for burial. Though some of her later roles, such as *Mata Hari* (1931, recommended by the author), certainly feature characters with connections to the vamp, we will, as with others here, be focusing on her work prior to 1930. There are other films from the 1920s that are accessible to the reader digitally, but should be noted to portray women in more tragic roles involving love, rather than roles where they purposefully manipulate their victims. Films such as *Love* (1927, based loosely on the novel *Anna Karenina*, 1878), show her versatility as well as her languid style, but do not fit as neatly in the vamp tradition as others, such as *The Kiss* (1929), which is in the suggested viewing list below.

Filmography

- *The Temptress* (1926)
- *Flesh and the Devil* (1926)
- *The Single Standard* (1929)
- *The Kiss* (1929)

Helen Louise Gardner
1884 – 1968

Helen Gardner as Cleopatra (1912), photograph by Robert Grau, *The Theatre of Science*, Broadway Publishing Company, New York.

Helen Gardner, circa 1912.

Born in New York, Helen Gardner was one of the earliest film actresses and her role as vamp characters predated Theda Bara (see separate entry) by at least four years. Unfortunately, she is largely forgotten today, primarily because her peak output period was in the earliest era of Hollywood filmmaking when quantity was more important than quality and numerous short films were the focus of many studios. Originally a stage actress, Gardner entered motion pictures in 1910 upon signing a contract with Vitagraph Studios (1897 – 1925), the most prolific studio of the time before it was purchased by Warner Bros. The majority of her output was in 1911 specifically, though she would star in a number of pictures until 1915. One of her crowning achievements was her portrayal of the character "Becky" in *Vanity Fair* (1911), followed by the formation of her production company, "Helen Gardner Picture Players," making her the first actor or actress in history to begin such a business. For a woman at the time to engage in such a venture was daring. She promoted her company with lavish advertisements and it was an early success with Gardner's production of *Cleopatra* (1912), where she played the title character roughly five years before Theda Bara. The film was later reissued when Bara's version was presented in an effort to capitalize both on Bara's fame as well as Gardner's claim to portraying the character earlier. Unfortunately, money issues apparently plagued Gardner's company after this production. In an era when bigger productions were becoming the norm, but were still costly gambles in comparison to shorter films, or "potboilers," which is where the majority of many a studios' finances lied. Gardner's pioneering attempts at bringing a focus on film as a more proper art form in the era is commendable, but sadly she has been overlooked for others, most likely due simply to the period in which she worked, which was a different industry. After her company folded in 1914, she returned to Vitagraph Studios briefly before working by 1915 for a short time with Universal. By 1916 her popularity waned, so she largely retired from acting except for some brief appearances, such as *Sandra* (1924). She married in 1902 shortly after turning eighteen, a move which garnered some gossip in Hollywood, especially after she and her husband became estranged, though they never divorced. Gardner lived a somewhat quiet, but comfortable life, until her death in Florida. Though she was known for playing strong, independent women in many of her films, including several of the vamp type, only a few representative examples survive that are accessible for the reader.

Filmography

- *The Show Girl* (1911)
- *Vanity Fair* (1911)
- *Cleopatra* (1912)

Louise Glaum
1888 – 1970

Louise Glaum portrait featured as a real photo postcard, circa 1920.

Louise Glaum on the cover of *Motion Picture Classic* Magazine, 1921.

Unlike some actresses of her generation, Louise Glaum found a successful transition out of film. Born near Baltimore, Maryland and one of four daughters, Glaum began acting in theater in the early 1900s. By 1908 she was frequently playing characters of the ingénue type (innocent and naïve), earning roughly $750 (adjusting for inflation in 2024) per week for her performances. As she said herself in an interview for *Movie Pictorial* in July of 1910, "I think every girl should be taught to earn her own living just as every boy is." Her turn of fate came at the death of her sister Margaret, who was nearly fourteen when she passed in 1911. This led Glaum to return to Los Angeles with her family, and after continuing work in ingénue roles locally, she began to peruse film studios in California. This quickly led to her first film role, starring in the Universal western comedy *When the Heart Calls* (1912). After this point she was noted for playing vamps in different films, including in the role of a seductive, French ballerina in *The Toast of Death*

(1915). Such roles earned her the nickname "The Spider Woman," though this comes from primarily one film, *Sex* (1920). A constant rumor also claims she was nicknamed "The Tiger Woman," but this only appears in modern texts and digital media. The nickname was indeed applied to women of the era at times, such as the real story of hammer murderess Clara Phillips (1898 – 1969), but in fact it comes from the Theda Bara (see separate entry) film *The Tiger Woman* (1917) and has nothing to do with Louise Glaum. Glaum was, however, in a film titled *The Leopard Woman* (1920), the reader should note. Regardless, known for her dark hair and dramatic style, Glaum was a noted expert at vamp portrayals prior to the rise of Theda Bara (see separate entry) and after. In 1916, for example, in the October 19th issue of *The Portsmouth Times* for her film *The Wolf Woman*, declared the "Greatest Vampire Picture of all," and of Glaum's portrayal of the character the writer of the script, Charles Gardner Sullivan (known commonly as C. Gardner, 1884 – 1965) said she was "living proof of the triumph of the flesh, in whose creed the lure of the physical was placed above the moral, spiritual or mental worth, and in whose incense-laden apartments the idol of sensuality replaced the crucifix or the family." Many of her films are sadly lost, including a few that were noted vamp roles, such as *Somewhere in France* (1916), but thankfully a few survive, including *The Wolf Woman*.

Filmography

- *The Wolf Woman* (1916)
- *Sex* (aka *The Spider Woman*, 1920)
- *The Leopard Woman* (1920)

Jetta Goudal
Julie Henriette Goudeket, 1891 – 1985

Image of Jetta Goudal from *Picture Play Magazine*, January 1927.

Jetta Goudal in a still from the American drama film
Salome of the Tenements (1925).

Born in Amsterdam to a wealthy Jewish diamond cutter named Wolf Mozes Goudeket (1860 – 1942), Jetta Goudal fled Europe for New York City in 1917 due to the devastation of the Great War (World War I), referring to herself as a "Parisienne" (a woman from Paris) to hide her background. She would deny her own father in press releases, where she stated she was the daughter of a lawyer born in Versailles in 1901, a statement held as fact until at least 1985. Her real father was later murdered at the Sobbidor extermination camp in Nazi-controlled Poland, a reality of which she never seemed to mention the rest of her life. Most of her relatives were victims of the Holocaust, in fact, with the exception of one daughter from her sister Bertha. Little is known about her feelings concerning her family, other than the great amount of secrecy she kept about her actual origins for many years after arriving in the United States. So good was she at hiding her identity that details on her origins were not made public until 1986, within a year of her death due to theatre historian Piet Hein Honig's (1957–2009) research. Theater is, in fact, where Goudal started acting, first in Europe, and then on Broadway in 1921 in *The Hero*. It is this particular play where she began to use her new name, pronouncing the 'J' in the French style (as zh) to hide her identity. Her first film role was a minor part in *Timothy's Quest* (1922) as a woman with tuberculosis and an alcoholic husband, though her name does not appear in the credits.

Moving to the West Coast she soon expanded her filmography, first as a "Chinese spy" in *The Bright Shawl* (1923), a minor role for which the New York Times declared her "impressive in her remarkable costumes." Her career then began to expand rapidly after her appearance as the character "Sonya Mendel" in *Salome of the Tenements* (1925), where she played a Jewess seeking her fortune through marriage, somewhat similar to the past she attempted to erase. After working on films for Cecil Blount DeMille (known typically as Cecil B., 1881 – 1959) she was involved in a lawsuit for breach of contract due; DeMille's claims that Goudal's difficult personality cost his studio thousands of dollars, a fact of which he could not prove, leading Goudal to win. This was, however, not her first lawsuit with a studio for her supposedly temperamental and, as some said, irrational behavior. After the DeMille case, which netted her $31,000 in damages in 1929 (over $500,000 in 2024), Goudal faced difficulty acquiring further work, her last film being the Western *Business and Pleasure* (1932). Famously in an interview for *Life* in 1984 she made light of the fact that she was difficult, stating: "I don't like being called a silent star. I was never silent." She retired after 1932, working with her husband in his business of interior design until she grew increasingly ill. Upon her death her husband, Harold Grieve (1901–1993) stated there would be no funeral, at his wife's request. Of her surviving films, two illustrate the vamp image most readily.

Filmography

- *Open All Night* (1924)
- *The Coming of Amos* (1925)

Barbara La Marr
Reatha Dale Watson, 1896 – 1926

Still from *Triling Women* (1922) starring Barbara La Marr and Ramon Novarro.

Portrait of Barbara La Marr, circa 1920.

Called "the girl who was too beautiful" by *Photoplay* in 1922, Barabara La Marr was a symbol of the excess of Hollywood in her era. Born in Yakima, Washington, La Marr's father was a writer, which led her family to frequently move along the West Coast of the United States. The impact of this upon her was great, as she developed an early interest in the arts, particularly writing, and was an avid reader. This interest was channeled into acting after she saw a play at the age of eight, and soon thereafter was a vaudeville dancer and eventually secured a role in a production of *Uncle Tom's Cabin* in 1904. Though her family was somewhat discouraging of her interest in film, her father eventually relented and she was permitted to move with her mother to Los Angeles, California by 1910, before he himself joined the family after securing a new position at a local newspaper. La Marr slowly entered into Hollywood, but initially starred in only small roles. Ever attracted to the turbulent life of the city, she was involved in numerous scandals. In 1913 at the age of sixteen, for example, as reported in *Photoplay* (June, 1922) she disappeared from her family's apartment, and was later discovered well but apparently "kidnapped" by her estranged half-sister and her boyfriend. After her parents moved to El Centro when her father received another job, La Marr, then seventeen, moved back to Los Angeles to continue on her path, abandoning her family and claiming to her friends upon her return that she had been married to a wealthy Arizona rancher and was left a widow. Because of her obsession with dancing and dance halls, engaging in frequent underage drinking, her father had her taken to juvenile court in an effort to bring her home. There, the judge famously stated to her, as reported in the same issue of *Photoplay* noted above: "You're too beautiful to be alone in a big city while you're so young. Go back to the country. Go back to your folks. You're too beautiful, my child. You don't understand where it might lead you." Back in Los Angeles, convincing her parents to follow, La Marr married a local garage manager who was already with a wife and child. The ensuing newspaper reports, as well as the manager's death after an attempt to reclaim his dignity by undergoing brain surgery for what was deemed a mental health issue, essentially blacklisted La Marr from working for any Hollywood studio and she returned to dancing and vaude-ville, changing her name to "Barbara La Marr" to distance herself from her controversial past.

Though she achieved some success after, she was no stranger to further controversy, involved in publicized marital scandals and eventually an invalid divorce to her supposedly fourth husband. During this time, she started to write once again, but this time for Hollywood, earning a $10,000 for Fox Film Corporation in 1920 for her efforts (roughly $160,000 in 2024). During this year, she became acquainted with Douglas

Elton Fairbanks Sr. (Douglas Elton Thomas Ullman, 1883 – 1939) on set of *The Mark of Zorro*. Encouraged by Fairbanks to try a screen test by 1921 she starred alongside the actor in *The Three Musketeers*, one of the most important blockbusters of the era. From this point her career was largely a flash. She starred in over twenty films from 1922 until 1926, and was noted for her "dark-eyed, exotic beauty" (*The Saturday Evening Post*, January 1924), but by 1925 opinions had changed. One critic writing in *Time* in April of 1925 said she was "not beautiful and certainly not a good actress," while another stated she "probably least deserves her distinction." Earlier controversies fueled her fame, and she was quite good at utilizing scandal, but by her death she had seemingly worn out her welcome as her true skill became more dubious. A good portion of her downfall was due to her declining health, which was caused partially by rampant drinking, extreme dieting, and a partying lifestyle. Stricken with pulmonary tuberculosis, she would eventually fall into a coma while working on her last film, *The Girl from Montmartre* (1926), dying of complications from her disease as well as nephritis. Though her career was primarily situated within a five-year period, La Marr played a number of vamp roles, but only a few of her films are accessible out of those that survived.

Filmography

- *The Prisoner of Zenda* (1922)
- *Trifling Women* (1922)
- *The White Moth* (1924)

Myrna Loy
Myrna Adele Williams, 1905 – 1993

Photograph of Myrna Loy from *Motion Picture Magazine*, September 1925.

MGM portrait, Everett Collection, circa 1930.

A famous name in the 1930s and 1940s especially, Myrna Loy started her career in the silent film industry, primarily in vamp roles. Born in Montana, Loy's grandparents came from Scotland and Sweden originally and became wealthy ranchers in the state. Her father worked a variety of jobs including banking and farm appraising, but Loy became connected with the performing arts at the age of twelve when she began dancing, eventually entering the Westlake School for Girls after her father died in the 1918 flu pandemic. By fifteen, while in public schooling, she started to perform in local theater productions in Los Angeles. While there, an early, though sometimes little-known, example of her fame came as the primary model for a 1922 sculpture entitled "Fountain of Education," which stood outside of her high school in Venice and went through a variety of adventures, such as a brief appearance in *Grease* (1978), and most recently in 2010 when the original was replaced by a bronze duplicate. Expanding her acting career, at eighteen Loy left school to support her family through her craft at

Grauman's Egyptian Theatre in Hollywood. There she starred in what were called "thematic prologues," short musical dance productions that would precede a film's presentation and were connected to the story the audience was about to see unveiled on screen. Photographs of her were eventually noticed by Rudolph Valentino (Rodolfo Pietro Filiberto Raffaello Guglielmi di Valentina d'Antonguella, 1895 – 1926), who approached Loy for a role in a film he was co-creating with his wife. Loy's photographs were taken by the then-famous portrait photographer Henry Waxman (1901 – 1963), whose work was found in many film magazines at the time, which led her popularity to rise.

Though she was eventually passed over for another actress to star as the lead in Valentino's *Cobra* (1925), in the same year she would play a vamp in a minor role in the film *What Price Beauty?* (1925). The now-lost production was unreleased for three years initially, but photographs of Loy in costume (see the image presented for her biography here), led to a contract with Warner Bros. as well as a name change for publicity purposes. In the silent era she starred in primarily vamp roles, in particular characters of Asian or Eurasian descent, a typecasting that would plague her into the 1930s in films such as *The Mask of Fu Manchu* (1932). By the end of the decade, however, Loy was one of Hollywood's most popular actresses, a status she would retain for most of her life. In spite of a few failed marriages, she was known later for portrayals of the "ideal wife" character in a variety of films and was noted for her wit. Very active in politics, including work for the United Nations, Loy passed the rest of her life in the public eye in a variety of ways, including acting, eventually dying during surgery due to an unstated illness (earlier in her life she had survived breast cancer, so cancer is a possibility). Her last appearance publicly was via television for her lifetime achievement award, which she did not have the strength to receive in-person. Her cremated remains were returned to her native Montana after her funeral. Though most of her acting fame came from her career in the 1930s and 1940s, some of Loy's titular vamp roles have survived and there are numerous photographs of other performances the reader can easily discover online.

Filmography

- *The Midnight Taxi* (1928)
- *The Desert Song* (1929)
- *The Black Watch* (1929)
- *The Squall* (1929)

Martha Mansfeld
Martha Ehrlich, 1899 – 1923

Cover of *Photoplay Magazine* featuring Martha Mansfeld, 1918.

Martha Mansfield, portrait by Alfred C. Johnston, 1918.

Though current information, including evidence from her passport application and death records, indicates Martha Mansfield was born in New York City, periodicals during her height of popularity in the 1920s consistently stated she was actually from Mansfield, Ohio, which is where she acquired her screen name after spending a portion of her childhood there. This story would find itself in biographies and articles for decades, but, in reality, New York was always her place of birth. Regardless, her father left her family while Mansfield was thirteen, and soon thereafter she began modeling and acting in theater for lower-budget Broadway productions and changed her name shortly thereafter. While modeling she was photographed by Alfred Cheney Johnston (1885 – 1971), who worked extensively for Broadway's "Ziegfeld Follies," elaborate Broadway musical, dance, and acting revues conceived by Florenz Edward Ziegfeld Jr. (1867 – 1932) and based on French models, which ran from roughly 1907 until 1930. Part of the Follies' repertoire was the "Ziegfeld Girls," dancers in lavish costumes who would perform in the audience and among elaborate sets. Mansfield would become one of the Ziegfeld Girls after starring in five films, including three comedy shorts, from 1917 to 1918, sometimes by the name "Martha Early." Some of her films were created at the studios of The Famous-Players Lasky Corporation, which would eventually become Paramount Pictures through several changes by 1927.

This connection to Famous Players gave Mansfield a route to Hollywood, where she moved by 1919, starring in the comedy *Civilian Clothes* (1920), followed by the role of "Millicent Carewe" in *Dr. Jekyll and Mr. Hyde* (1920). Juggling film roles with the vaudeville circuit, Mansfield signed a contract with Fox Film Corporation in 1923. Her career was advancing quickly, but a tragic accident ended her short life in November of 1923 while filming *The Warrens of Virginia* (1924). At some point during the production when Mansfield was retiring to her car to relax, a thrown match ignited her costume, engulfing her in flames within her vehicle. Though she was initially saved, burns covered large portions of her body and she died in a hospital of various complications. Stories have varied over the years as to how the death actually occurred, one publication, *The No-Tobacco Educator* from February of 1924, stating that a match of a "smoker" was tossed upon the ground, suggesting Mansfield brushed over it as she walked to her car, whereas others erroneously claimed Mansfield herself was smoking. Regardless of how the incident occurred, it brought about a quick end of a rising star whose abilities were only just gaining significant recognition. Though she portrayed a number of characters and only a few of the vamp type, or thematically close to it, thankfully two representative films have survived.

Filmography

- *Is Money Everything?* (1923)
- *The Silent Command* (1923)

Nita Naldi
Mary Nonna Dooley, 1894 – 1961

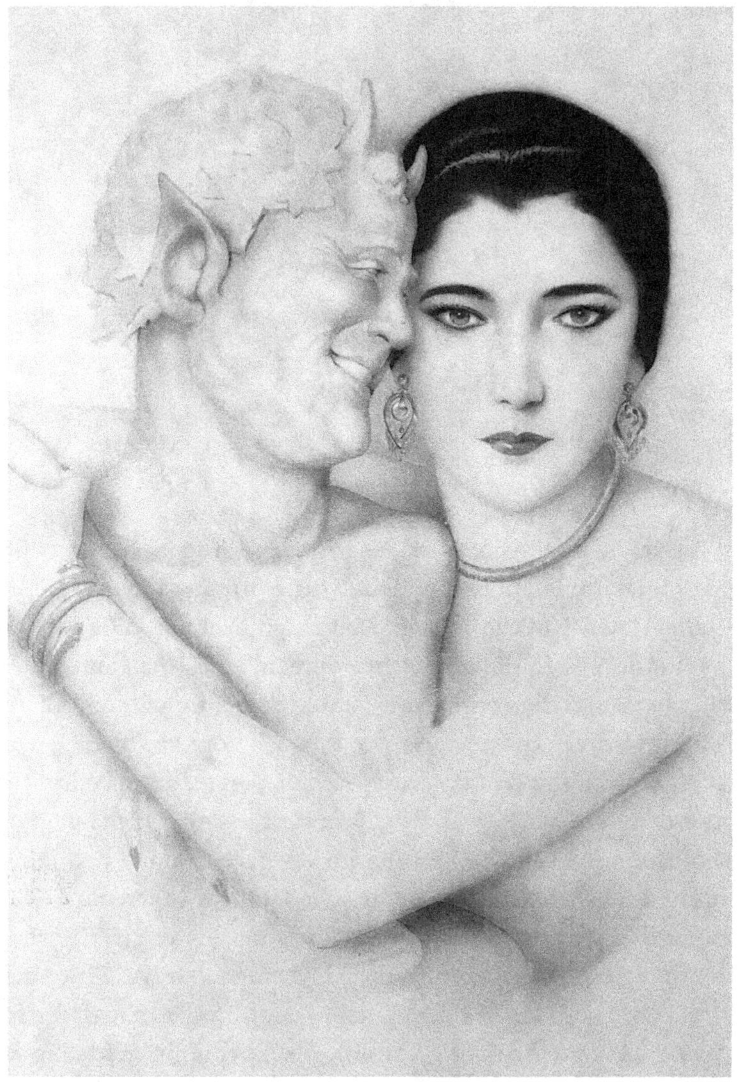

Nita Naldi with a statue of a faun, illustrated by Alberto Vargas.

Nita Naldi on page 25 of the December 1922 issue of *Photoplay.*

Nita Naldi, who maintained a fairly vague story of her early life as she became more popular, was born in a tenement in Harlem, which at the time housed a significant Irish immigrant population. Both of her parents were, in fact, Irish, and young Naldi was raised in a relatively stable home, though four of her siblings would die at early ages, two before she herself was born. Her family was devoutly Catholic, and she was educated at the private school Holy Angels in New Jersey, which her great aunt founded in 1879. By 1910, however, her family had fallen into various tragedies including deaths from tuberculosis and her father leaving in 1910, though he continued to live close to Naldi. By 1915, when her mother died from a stroke, Nita Naldi was living with her at the Regina Angelorum Catholic Home for Working Women. Taking various jobs, including modeling, to assist in the care of her two remaining siblings, only one of which would survive into adulthood, Naldi at some point began to enter vaudeville, though details on this are scant as she herself seemed to have ignored several stages of her life in interviews. Her stage name, though, is known to have come from a roommate she lived with in Manhattan after leaving her family, named "Maria Naldi," who she claimed was her sister, along with claiming she was of various backgrounds including Italian and Spanish. Later scholars have suggested the pair may have been lovers, but this has not been verified. Regardless, by 1918 she was in her first known stage production for The Shubert Organization (formed in 1900), *The Passing Show of 1918*, where she was a chorus girl, in particular for Act 1 in "My Vampire Girl." This, and other roles, would establish her as a theater vamp by the beginning of the 1920s, and she had some small involvement with Ziegfeld Follies (see entry on Martha Mansfield for more information) as well. Other than one clear stage credit, however, this connection is uncertain, other than the illustration that started this section, which was completed by Joaquin Alberto Vargas y Chávez (known commonly as Alberto Vargas, 1896 – 1982), famed pin-up artist who did a number of works for the Follies.

Eventually, Naldi was cast as the character "Gina" in her first verified film role for *Dr. Jekyll and Mr. Hyde* (1920). In it, Gina "Who Faced Her World Alone" dances on stage in vamp fashion, which excites the hidden evil within Dr. Jekyll. How she came upon this role is still uncertain, but regardless Naldi's depiction of Gina led to further roles culminating soon thereafter in a contract with The Famous Players–Lasky Corporation (see entry on Martha Mansfield for more information) for the film *Blood and Sand* (1922), where she co-starred with Rudolph Valentino (Rodolfo Pietro Filiberto Raffaello Guglielmi di Valentina d'Antonguella, 1895 – 1926). Still considered her greatest achievement in film and her most successful production in her career, it solidified her as a film vamp, which all but ruined her career for the rest of the decade. In the March 1925 issue of *Motion Picture*, for example, she supposedly co-authored with Barabar La Marr (see separate entry) the two-page article "This Business of Being a Vampire," though there is no proof either of them ever had any hand in it. In it, she supposedly stated: "Every woman is potentially a vampire. In an impulsive moment, weary of the monotony of her life, she may decide to take a fling at something different, and this fling may ruin her life." The publicity around her vamp characters, as well as discussions of her lack of marketability after *Blood and Sand* and discussions in the press concerning her drinking and weight, slowly whittled away at what popularity Naldi had managed to gather. It became clear that her connections to Valentino allowed her to retain her power as a co-star, but once he quit Paramount (originally The Famous-Players Lasky Coporation) in 1924 she lost this edge, in spite of attempting to continue in his short-lived studio venture of Ritz-Carlton Pictures Incorporated.

By 1925 she starred in her last American film *What Price Beauty?* (not released until 1928, see entry on Myrna Loy for more information) but barely received any recognition and her career quickly dissipated. She would star in three films in Europe, including an odd casting as a vamp-like schoolmistress in Alfred Hitchcock's lost second film *The Mountain Eagle* (1926) and in 1929 married the mysterious J. Searle Barclay, of whom only one surviving photograph exists. Though they were married for twenty-five years before his death in 1945, very little is known about him. Greatly affected by the Great Depression, Naldi declared bankruptcy in 1933 while living in the Plaza Hotel in New York. Though she would star in various stage roles in the 1940s and 1950s, including one legendary stage performance of Kipling's poem "A Fool There Was," declining health eventually made her absent from the public eye. She later died from heart failure. Thankfully, though the majority of her films are lost, some of the more important examples where she played vamp characters survived.

Filmography

- *Dr. Jekyll and Mr. Hyde* (1920)
- *Blood and Sand* (1922)
- *The Ten Commandments* (1923)
- *Cobra* (1925)

Pola Negri
Barbara Apolonia Chalupec, 1897 — 1987

Pola Negri on the cover *Picture Play Magazine*, March 1923.

Pola Negri in *Screenland,* December 1923.

The most famous film star from out of Poland internationally, arguably even today, Pola Negri was widely recognized in the vamp era and maintained a strong following up until her death. Negri was born in Lipno, which at the time was part of the Russian Empire as the "Polish Kingdom" (Królestwo Polskie), a semi-independent state. At the time of her birth revolutionary activity and revolts were widespread in Eastern Europe, including what would eventually become the country of Poland by 1918. After her father, who was a Romani-Slovak, was arrested in 1902 by the Russians for revolutionary activity, she and her mother lived in poverty. In spite of this, her education and skill in ballet would eventually lead her to debut in a part of *Swan Lake* performed in Warsaw in 1908. After a solo role in the comedy *Coppélia* (originally debuted in 1870), however, she suffered a bought of tuberculosis. During this time, she adapted the stage name "Pola Negri," based on the name of Italian poet Ada Negri (1870 – 1945), as well as the diminutive form of her own first name. After recovering from her disease,

Negri was accepted into the "Warsaw Theatre Directorate" (Warszawskie Teatry Rządowe) and starred as "Aniela" in the play *Maiden Vows* (*Śluby panieńskie*, first debuted in 1833) in 1912. When she debuted in this role at the "Little Theatre" (Teatr Mały) in Warsaw, she first used her new stage name. Though the play was not well-received, Negri would nonetheless gain more roles and eventually entered film for the first time in Poland. The film was *A Slave to Her Senses* (*Niewolnica Zmysłów*, 1914), directed by Jan Pawłowski (1878 – 1936). Now lost, other than some publicity stills and posters, Negri starred as a dancer, a skill she would utilize as part of her allure in her roles.

In this early period, her most important film, arguably, was *The Beast* (*Bestia*, 1917), directed by Aleksander Hertz (1879 – 1928). This film in particular gained her international recognition including in the United States, where it was distributed under the title of *The Polish Dancer*. In Germany, the film was also a success, and provided her with an opportunity to enter the theatre and film industry in Berlin. Though Negri found herself largely playing smaller roles, by the end of the 1910s she starred in bigger productions, such as *The Eyes of the Mummy Ma* (*Die Augen der Mumie Ma*, 1918). Her presence in Europe was even noticed by Charlie Chaplin (Sir Charles Spencer Chaplin, 1889 – 1977), and she was offered a contract in 1921 via Paramount Pictures, then known as The Famous-Lasky Players Corporation (see entry on Martha Mansfield for more information). This move transformed into a legendary rivalry with Gloria Swanson (1899 – 1983), who attempted to subdue her foreign rival's power. *The New York Times* noted in 1925, for example, that "of all the screen actresses one sees working here, Pola Negri is the most interesting." At this time, however, her exotic image, as pushed by Famous-Lasky, was wearing thin on audiences, partially due to her affairs, including one with Charlie Chaplin and another with Rudolph Valentino (Rodolfo Pietro Filiberto Raffaello Guglielmi di Valentina d'Antonguella, 1895 – 1926), followed by a rebound marriage in France that occurred a little over eight months after Valentino's death. Now in the sound period, and after releasing a film in United Kingdom, she later returned to Hollywood for *A Woman Commands* (1932), and from there starred in films in France and Germany. The latter led her to have some connection with the Nazi Party, as Adolf Hitler (1889 – 1945) considered one of her German vehicles, *Mazurka* (1935), one of his favorite films. This even led to a well-publicized rumor that Negri had an affair with Hitler, a false claim that later led her to a successful lawsuit against the magazine that published the original story, *Pour Vous* (1928 – 1940). She then fled to France, later Portugal during the Nazi Occupation, and eventually returned to the United States by 1945, doing a tour of the song "Paradise," for which she had received much acclaim in the film *A Woman Commands*. Largely retiring from the public eye, Negri would eventually play her final role in the Walt Disney mystery *The Moon-Spinners* (1964). She hoped this particular role would have won her an Oscar nomination, a distinction she ironically lost years prior when Gloria Swanson was nominated for Best Actress for her role in the film *Sunset Boulevard* (1950), which Negri herself declined prior. Entering retirement, she would eventually die from pneumonia and complications from an untreated brain tumor in 1987. In spite of her disappearance from the public eye at the end of her life, her exotic, and lanky build, was the material of legend and Negri was a true public spectacle who created fashion trends and images that have still persisted. Due to her popularity, luckily a number of her films that illustrate the vamp, including earlier ones, survive.

Filmography

- *The Beast* (*Bestia*, 1917)
- *Mania* (*Mania. Die Geschichte einer Zigarettenarbeiterin*, 1918)
- *The Eyes of Mummy Ma* (*Die Augen der Mumie Ma*, 1918)
- *Carmen* (known also as *Gypsy Blood*, 1918)
- *Madame DuBarry* (known also as *Passion*, 1919)
- *Sumurun* (1920)
- *Arme Violetta* (also known as *The Red Peacock*, 1920)
- *Sappho* (also known as *Mad Love*, 1920)
- *Bella Donna* (1923)
- *A Woman of the World* (1925)
- *The Way of Lost Souls* (also known as *The Woman He Scorned*, 1929)

Asta Nielsen
Asta Sofe Amalie Nielsen, 1881 – 1972

Asta Nielsen as Stella on the set of the danish silent movie *The Black Dream* (*Den sorte drøm*, 1911).

Asta Nielsen publicity photo, circa 1920-1930.

Born to an impoverished family in Copenhagen, Denmark, Asta Nielsen moved to Sweden when she was younger, where she lived until the age of seven, as her father tried to find stable work, eventually settling back in Copenhagen, but he would die when she was almost the age of fourteen. By the age of eighteen, Nielsen was accepted into the Royal Danish Theatre (Det Kongelige Teater), where she was recognized for her striking tenor voice. At twenty-one she was pregnant with her daughter Jesta, though the father remained unknown, and this affected her career at the time. She attempted on numerous occasions to enter the theater industry in Copenhagen, but was only featured in minor roles, even touring Norway and Sweden though there is no record she achieved any real success critically there, some critics praising her physique but finding her voice a hindrance to real success. Film would be her true calling, though it largely occurred by accident when she starred in Danish director Urban Gad's (Peter Urban Bruun Gad, 1879 – 1947) low-budget film *The Abyss* (*Afgrunden*, 1910). An unexpected success, the film gained international recognition through the popularity of Danish erotic melodramas at the time, as well as the monopoly distribution system, entering the United States in 1912 as *Woman Always Pays*. In the film, Nielsen performs her famous "gaucho dance," a highly erotic moment that even by today's standards may seem rather lurid, and which was censored in some cuts of the film, including the third Swedish version. Though it has been stated by some sources that Nielsen's films were censored in the United States, there is no clear record of this, and her seeming lack of popularity in the country was primarily owed to the impact of World War I on Germany's film distribution. In the United States, simply put, German films were usually blocked from import because of anti-German tensions during the war.

Nielsen would make four more films with Gad, whom she married in 1912, and her popularity led her to enter the film industry in Germany. She was provided with far more control than other actresses of her time, and became an international sensation, especially through control of her "Asta Nielsen Series" (a collection of her various films provided through distribution). This situation would change when more director-focused productions emerged by the end of the 1920s. Though her first marriage would end in 1919, and she had four more, the bulk of her film career continued in Germany until the sound era. Her final film was *Impossible Love* (*Unmögliche Liebe*, 1932), a role for which she was considered "rediscovered" by at least one critic. When she was approached by Adolf Hitler (1889 – 1945) to reenter the industry because of the potential political power of her film presence, she declined and eventually returned to Belgium by 1937, understanding the implications of the Nazi dictator's discussion. She would later provide some assistance, indirectly, to Jews during the Holocaust. The remainder of Nielsen's life would remain relatively quiet, though she became famous for her paintings, which would connect her with Danish art collector Christian Freede (date of birth approximately 1892, date of death unknown), whom she married when she was the age of eighty, a much-celebrated moment of late-life happiness in the press. When Nielsen died in 1972, only film historians truly remembered her. Known in her time as "the Duse of film" ("die Duse des Kinos") after famed Italian stage actress Eleonora Giulia Amalia Duse (1858 – 1924), Nielsen was noted for her more naturalistic approach to acting, a sharp departure from the overly theatrical style that typified the early silent period in which she became a star. Some of her most important vamp-type roles have survived, but it should be noted that Nielsen was extremely gifted and portrayed a number of notable roles, such as Mary Magdalene in *I.N.R.I* (1923), and often of tragic women, such as *Downfall* (*Der Absturz*, 1923). One of her most critically acclaimed roles was in *Hamlet* (1921), where she played the title character as a woman masquerading as a man, a depiction that is still discussed today. In spite of the variety of her work, however, the selection provided here is of her roles as close to the vamp as possible, including some that relate to the typical image.

Poster for *Hamlet* starring Asta Nielsen by Franz A. Peffer, circa 1920.

Filmography

- *The Abyss* (*Afgruden*, 1910)
- *The Black Dream* (*Den sorte drøm*, 1911)
- *Ballet Dancers* (*Balletdanserinden*, 1911)
- *The Traitress* (*Die Verräterin*, 1911)
- *Earthspirit* (*Erdgeist*, 1923)

Anna May Wong

Wong Liu Tsong, 黃柳霜

January 3, 1905 – February 3, 1961

Chinese-American actress Anna May Wong on the cover of *Liangyou* (*The Young Companion*), issue #16. Published on June 30, 1927.

Anna May Wong in *Picture Play Magazine*, May 1923.

Born in Chinatown in Los Angeles as Huang Liu Shuang, which means literally "Yellow Willow Frost," Anna May Wong was a versatile and famous actor in the silent through early sound periods, in addition to some later roles before her death. She was the first Chinese American actor to achieve worldwide acclaim and exemplified a character type that later was known as the "dragon lady," which can be considered an Asian form of the vamp. Other actresses in the era presented such characters in mimicked fashion, an approach that is not politically correct today, but Wong was its primary form originally. At the time of her early childhood, condemnation of Chinese Americans was widespread in the United States. Her grandfather was part of the large Chinese immigrant population that entered the country via California in the late 19th century during the Gold Rush, connected to mining and the railroad industry, and her family witnessed anti-Chinese policies in politics such as the "Chinese Exclusion Act" of 1882. Young Anna May assisted her family in their laundromat and like many before her encountered racism in all of its ugliness. This eventually led to her entrance into a Chinese Mission School at the Chinese Congregational Church in Los Angeles, partially to avoid antagonism from other children at a local school from which she was removed. During this time, she became interested in acting due to the shift in filmmaking from New York to California, changing her name to Anna May Wong as a combination of her Chinese heritage and American identity. She soon accepted her first role as an extra in *The Red Lantern* (1919), an epic film starring Alla Nazimova (1879 – 1945, who herself starred in some vamp-type roles), concerning the Boxer Rebellion, for Metro Pictures Corporation (1915 – 1924), a precursor to Metro-Goldwyn-Mayer. In the film she portrayed a simple lantern bearer, a brief moment that is difficult to locate during the scene of the "Red Lantern Festival" nearly an hour into the film.

Though uncredited, this role was her entrance into Hollywood and was soon followed by others, including her first leading role in the Technicolor production *The Toll of the Sea* (1922), an adaptation of the opera *Madama Butterfly* (debuted in 1904), itself an adaptation of the short story "Madame Butterfly" (1898) by John Luther Long (1861 – 1927). Due to typecasting in roles typical to Asian actors, Wong attempted to create her own production company named "Anna May Wong Productions" in 1924, hoping to make films about Chinese legends, but the business was soon dissolved due to underhanded business dealings of a partner involved in the proceedings, Forrest B. Creighton (date of birth and death unknown). By the late 1920s, tired of supporting roles and the status of Chinese actors in the industry due to concerns of miscegenation, as well as non-Chinese actors playing as Chinese characters, Wong left Hollywood for Europe. Rules about miscegenation were a central problem for Wong, in fact, because they restricted her ability to play leading roles, typically leaving her relegated to typecasting as a woman who would be cast away by the leading male character of the film. In Europe she found more success in films such as *Song* (*Schmutziges Geld* in German, 1928), where she plays the title character, a tragic woman who falls in love with a man who saves her, only to be betrayed before he realizes, too late, how she truly loves him. After an attempt at working with the Hong Kong Film industry in 1928, she returned to Hollywood to star in various roles, as well as finding fame through numerous stage appearances. Her final role as a Chinese villain was as "Princess Ming Loy" in *Daughter of the Dragon* (1931), one of the many "Fu Manchu" pictures of the era. Following this, she starred in the critically acclaimed *Shanghai Express* (1932) and later toured China in 1936. Among other ventures she was an advocate for Chinese refugees during World War II and, later, was the first Asian-American with a lead role in a television program in the series *The Gallery of Madame Liu-Tsong*, which ran for a single season in 1951. Unlike many actresses presented in this biography section, Anna May Wong had a relatively fruitful career throughout her life, though sometimes with stereotyped roles, until her death of a heart attack in 1961. More recently, in 2022 specifically, her face was featured on a United States quarter, making her the first Asian American in history to receive this honor. Though her fame developed to a great extent in the 1930s and beyond, and the majority of her "dragon lady" roles are from this era, earlier examples of her work with some elements of the vamp have survived. The reader should note that late work more easily exemplifies this tradition, but elements can be found in the following films.

Filmography

- *The Thief of Bagdad* (1924)
- *Old San Francisco* (1927)
- *Piccadilly* (1929)

Acknowledgments

Special thanks to all family, friends, and students who read earlier versions of the story long before I decided to publish it. At this point I regret not keeping track of everyone's names so I'll leave this general so no one feels left out. Thanks to all of you.

Stanley Stepanic
August, 2024

About the Author

Stanley Stepanic is an assistant professor of Slavic languages and literatures in the Slavic Department at the University of Virginia. Along with courses on the Polish language and Eastern European film, he teaches a popular course on the history of vampires called "Dracula." *A Vamp There Was* utilizes some of his research. He grew up near Pittsburgh, Pennsylvania, and currently lives with his wife and daughter in Charlottesville.

Image Credits

Frances Benjamin Johnston Photograph Collection. Library of Congress, Prints & Photographs Division, [Reproduction number: LC-DIG-csas-06095]. https://www.loc.gov/item/2017891829/

Image as it appeared in The History of the City of Fredericksburg, Virginia, By Silvanus Jackson Quinn, 1908, page 296, PUBLIC DOMAIN. https://tile.loc.gov/image-services/iiif/public:gdcmassbookdig:historyofcityoff00quin:historyofcityoff00quin_0365/full/pct:100.0/0/default.jpg

The Highway Inn. Frances Benjamin Johnston Photograph Collection, Library of Congress, Prints & Photographs Division, [Reproduction number: LC-DIG-csas-05912] https://www.loc.gov/item/2017891650/

The Bradford Building. Image as it appeared in The History of the City of Fredericksburg, Virginia By Silvanus Jackson Quinn, 1908, page 42, PUBLIC DOMAIN. https://tile.loc.gov/image-services/iiif/public:gdcmassbookdig:historyofcityoff00quin:historyofcityoff00quin_0057/full/pct:100.0/0/default.jpg

Postcard from approximately 1920 to 1926 of the Princess Anne Hotel, Public Domain

A watercolor from 1904 by Eugène Decisy (1866 – 1936) based upon the work of Paul Albert Laurens (1870 – 1934). https://commons.wikimedia.org/wiki/File:La_Morte_amoureuse_-_Sa_t%C3%AAte_retomba_en_arri%C3%A8re,_mais_elle_m%27en-tourait_toujours_de_ses_bras.jpg

Phillip Burne-Jones "The Vampire" from 1897. https://commons.wikimedia.org/wiki/File:Philip_Burne-Jones_-_The_Vampire.jpg

Cover of *A Fool There Was* from author's own collection. Public domain.

Katherine Kaelred Seated On Bench. Moffett Photo. Bain News Service. Library of Congress. https://www.loc.gov/pictures/item/2014684756/

Alice Eis and Bert French in Robert G. Vignola's film *The Vampire* (1913). https://commons.wikimedia.org/wiki/File:The_Vampire_(1913).jpg

Original movie poster for *A Fool There Was* (1915), created by Arthur Dickson (Fox Film Corporation). https://commons.wikimedia.org/wiki/File:Fooltherewas1915movieposter.jpg

Theda Bara. Public Domain. Attribution: https://www.flickr.com/photos/likeabalalaika/3749417056

A Fool There Was (1915) original poster. Public Domain. https://jenikirbyhis

Image Credits

tory.getarchive.net/amp/media/a-fool-there-was-1915-film-original-poster-71d492

Ad for *The Vampire* (1915). Public Domain. https://commons.wikimedia.org/wiki/File:Petrova_Vampire_ad.jpg

Fascinatin' Vamp. Scan from Author's collection. Public domain.

Advertisement for the lost silent film *Trifling Women*, October 1922. https://commons.wikimedia.org/wiki/File:Triflingwoman-newspaperad1922.png

Vampire Girl, Coles Phillips (1880-1927). *Life Magazine.* 1925. Public Domain. http://www.thekellycollection.org/a_phil01.htm

Sheet music cover: "The Siren's Song." Illustrated cover with image of Theda Bara / Barbelle. *The Siren's Song* (Motion picture : 1919). Margaret Herrick Library, Academy of Motion Picture Arts and Sciences. https://digitalcollections.oscars.org/digital/collection/p15759coll6/id/2426

Josephine Baker in *La Sirène des Tropiques* by G. Rader, c. 1927, chromolithograph on paper, from the National Portrait Gallery. https://commons.wikimedia.org/wiki/File:Josephine_Baker_in_La_Sir%C3%A8ne_des_Tropiques_by_G._Rader,_c._1927,_chromolithograph_on_paper,_from_the_National_Portrait_Gallery_-_NPG-NPG_86_66.jpg

Josephine Baker, portrait by Henri Manuel, circa 1920. Public Domain. https://commons.wikimedia.org/wiki/File:Jos%C3%A9phine_Baker_-_photo_Henri_Manuel.jpg

Theda Bara. *The She-Devil.* Picture is unedited original from creator. https://commons.wikimedia.org/wiki/File:Theda_Bara_-_The_She-Devil_01.jpg License: https://creativecommons.org/licenses/by-sa/4.0/deed.en

Portrait of Theda Bara with hands held under her chin by Orval Hixon. 1921. https://commons.wikimedia.org/wiki/File:Theda_Bara_1921_Orval_Hixon.jpg

Elisabeth Bergner. Image Used By Permission from Flickr User rauter25. NO changes have been made other than resizing and author does not endorse the usage. https://www.flickr.com/photos/27556454@N07/3372659772 Commons License: https://creativecommons.org/licenses/by-sa/2.0/

Billy Rose Theatre Division, The New York Public Library. "Elizabeth Bergner" *The New York Public Library Digital Collections.* 1850 - 2020. https://digitalcollections.nypl.org/items/510d47d9-ffab-a3d9-e040-e00a18064a99

Olive Borden. Public Domain. https://ia801301.us.archive.org/BookReader/BookReaderImages.php?zip=/12/items/photoplay3031movi/photoplay3031movi_jp2.zip&file=photoplay3031movi_jp2/photoplay3031movi_0470.jp2&id=photoplay3031movi&scale=2&rotate=0

Olive Borden. Image from *Cine Mundial Magazine*, March 1929. https://

archive.org/stream/cinemundial14unse#page/n257/mode/1up, Public Domain, https://commons.wikimedia.org/w/index.php?curid=66595144

Clara Bow. Lobby card for the film *It* (1927). https://commons.wikimedia.org/wiki/File:It_(1927_lobby_card,_Clara_Bow_-_2).jpg

Clara Bow. Photograph by J. Willis Sayre, 1928. https://commons.wikimedia.org/wiki/File:Clara_Bow,_film_actress_(SAYRE_4377).jpg

Lili Damita. https://commons.wikimedia.org/wiki/File:Lily_Damita_1928-1929_Alexander_Binder_001.jpg

Lili Damita. Image from Cine Mundial, December 1928. https://commons.wikimedia.org/wiki/File:Lili_Damita_CM1229.jpg

Lya de Putti. Photo by Alexander Binder. https://commons.wikimedia.org/wiki/File:Lya_de_Putti_1927-1929_Alexander_Binder_1028-3.gif

Still from the American silent drama film *The Sorrows of Satan* (1926) with Lya De Putti, on page 37 of the July 1926 *American Beauties* magazine. https://commons.wikimedia.org/wiki/File:The_Sorrows_of_Satan_(1926)_-_3.jpg

Kay Francis. *New Movie Magazine,* December 1929. https://archive.org/details/newmoviemagazine01weir/page/2/mode/2up?view=theater

Kay Francis (1905-1968) from Modern Screen, February 1931. https://commons.wikimedia.org/wiki/File:Kay_Francis_1931.jpg

Greta Garbo. 1920. Library of Congress. https://www.loc.gov/resource/gdcwdl.wdl_11626/?r=-0.986,-0.132,2.972,1.195,0

Greta Garbo in 1925, by Alexander Binder. https://commons.wikimedia.org/wiki/File:Greta_Garbo_1925,_by_Alexander_Binder.jpg

Helen Gardner as Cleopatra. 1912. Robert Grau (1914) *The Theatre of Science,* Broadway publishing company, New York. https://commons.wikimedia.org/wiki/File:Helen_Gardner_as_Cleopatra.jpg

Helen Gardner, circa 1912. Photographer unknown. J168040 U.S. Copyright Office. https://commons.wikimedia.org/wiki/File:Actress_Helen_Gardner_c1912.jpg

Louise Glaum. *Motion Picture Classic Magazine,* November 1920. https://commons.wikimedia.org/wiki/File:Motion_Picture_Classic,_November_1920.jpg

Louise Glaum. Real Photo Postcard, 1920s. https://immortalephemera.com/wp-content/gallery/1920s-real-photo-postcards/thumbs/thumbs_louise-glaum-a.jpg

Jetta Goudal. *Picture Play Magazine,* January 1927. https://archive.org/details/PicturePlay192701

Barbara La Marr. Still from the American film *Trifling Women* (1922). https://garystockbridge617.getarchive.net/media/trifling-women-sayre-14795-6639a8

Image Credits

Portrait of Barbara La Marr, circa 1920. https://commons.wikimedia.org/wiki/File:Barbara_LaMarr.jpg

Photograph of Myrna Loy as appeared in *Motion Picture* magazine, September 1925. https://commons.wikimedia.org/wiki/File:Myrna-Loy-1925.jpg

Myrna Loy. MGM portrait, Everett Collection, circa 1930. https://commons.wikimedia.org/wiki/File:MYRNALoy.jpg

Martha Mansfield. *Photoplay Magazine*, 1918. https://commons.wikimedia.org/wiki/File:Martha_Mansfield_Photoplay_Magazine_1918.png

Nita Naldi with a statue of a faun, illustrated by Alberto Vargas. https://commons.wikimedia.org/wiki/File:Nita_Naldi_with_a_statue_of_a_faun,_illustrated_by_Alberto_Vargas.jpg

Actress Nita Naldi on page 25 of the December 1922 *Photoplay*. https://archive.org/details/photoplayvolume222chic

Pola Negri on the cover *Picture Play Magazine*, March 1923 https://picryl.com/media/pictureplay1923-03-cover-pola-negri-84e7f3

Pola Negri in *Screenland,* December *1923*. http://archive.org/stream/screenland08unse#page/n235/mode/1up

Asta Nielsen as Stella on the set of the danish silent movie *The Black Dream* (OT *Den sorte drøm*). 1911. https://commons.wikimedia.org/wiki/File:Asta_Nielsen.jpg

Asta Nielsen publicity photo, circa 1920-1930. https://digitalcollections.universiteitleiden.nl/view/item/1893892

1920 circa Franz A. Peffer Poster for *Hamlet*, Asta Nielsen, Art-Film, Druck von Meissner & Buch. https://commons.wikimedia.org/wiki/File:1920_circa_Franz_A._Peffer_Poster_for_Hamlet,_Asta_Nielsen,_Art-Film,_Druck-_von_Meissner_%26_Buch.jpg

Chinese-American actress Anna May Wong on the cover of *Liangyou* (The Young Companion), issue #16. Published on June 30, 1927. https://commons.wikimedia.org/wiki/File:Liangyou_016_cover_-_Anna_May_Wong.png